ALREADY TAKEN 2

Already Taken 2

This novel is a work of fiction. Any references to real people, events, establishments, or locales are intended only to give the fiction a sense of reality and authenticity. Other names, characters, and incidents occurring in the work are either the product of the author's imagination or are used fictitiously, as those fictionalized events and incidents that involve real persons. Any character that happens to share the name of a person who is an acquaintance of the author, past or present, is purely coincidental and is in no way intended to be an actual account involving that person.

ISBN- 13: 978-0-9895370-2-5

ISBN- 10: 0-98953-702-1

LCCN: 2013944350

First Printing November 2013

Printed in the United States of America

Editors: Jamie Pender and Shanovia Brown
Typesetting: Jamie Pender

Cover Design by Brittani Williams
www.tspubcreative.com

Acknowledgements

First, I'd like to thank the Lord for blessing me with the talent of writing. You really helped me with this one. Already Taken 2 is/was *undoubtedly* the hardest book I've ever written. I agonized over this book for nearly a year. Now it's finally here! Thank you for getting me through it!

My mother, thank you for your unconditional love and countless late-night conversations. My father, if one was to look up the definition of a strong man, they would find your picture next to it. You are the rock of this family, definitely. I know this will sound sappy, but y'all are my heroes. Because of that, I want to be *your* hero, too. I swear that I will make good on everything I've promised y'all. Because of y'all, I've *never* went without. Allow me to do the same for y'all. Love y'all more than I can possibly acknowledge here.

My son, DJ, I do this to ensure that you have everything you deserve! I love you! You are definitely the love of my life!

My kid sis Jyun—better known to the world as Nicole Red—thanks for taking those nightly walks with me. You let me vent my frustrations about the book and even offered your input. Thanks a lot!

Grandma Chick (1927-2012), it's almost that time of the year again… when I lost you. I always get nostalgic as the date nears… I took your words to heart, and I promise that I will *always* help family.

To my family—Grandma Lizzie (one of—if not the most—selfless person I know), Grandpa Walter, Aunt Annette, Uncle Darryl, Uncle Tony, Aunt Gena, Aunt Bev,

Uncle Tommy, Aunt Sondra, Aunt Deb, and Uncle Allen. My cousins Jonique, Monique, Mick, Darnell, Amanda, Chas, Kim, Keith, Killer, Kayla, Quin, Tesha, and Jordan. So many of y'all to name, and I know I left out a few of you, but I love y'all!!!

Miss Nakea Murray (affectionately known as My Miss Nakea). I can finally acknowledge you properly. You have taught me darn near everything I know and honestly, I know if it wasn't for you I doubt I would've made it this far. I love you and am so thankful for you taking time out of your day to teach me the game. It's been a while since we spoke. I miss you!

My best friend and my son's Godparents: Katrina Kent-Saunders and AJ Saunders! I love y'all, my lil' Maliyah, and Baby AJ (fingers crossed it's a boy)! We're almost ten years strong, huh? Time flies!

The bestie and my assistant, Chelle!!! It seems like it was just yesterday we were talking about getting out of Raleigh and moving to ATL. Now we did it! Making our dreams come true! Love you, girl! 2014 is ours!!! We've come too far for it not to be!

My cousin Jonique!!! I can't wait until your book comes out and we can make this a family affair! I love the conversations that we have darn near everything—from our texting, calling, to them durn voice memos we like to send. LOL I'm so glad I moved to Raleigh and we got the chance to get closer. Love you!!!

One of the hardest working authors in the game and my bestie, Jade Jones! You are definitely a force to be reckoned with and an author that EVERYONE needs to be aware of! It's great to have someone that understands my trials and tribulations. I can vent to you and you actually understand my POV. For that, I'm so appreciative.

My godsister, my Jenni-oneesama. I view you not only as an older sister, but definitely as a mentor. I'm thankful for all of your guidance throughout the years and I'm so glad to have met you in my lifetime. I am still hoping that N. L. Armitage will make a comeback because I know that you'll definitely be the next BIG thing!

My cuz, Denisha, I miss you! We've known each other since 3rd grade and I can say that you've always been there for me. Thank you. Love you!

My Titia-ann. I remember you were one of the first people to read the original 'Already Taken' and offer me feedback. Thank you. I'm always grateful for your sound advice (on the rare occasions when you're around to give it. LOL) I'm ready for all that stuff we were talking about. That—and I quote—*Girlfriends, Waiting to Exhale, Why Did I Get Married?, Best Man Holiday*, type ish! LOL

My 'nelle! I'm so glad that you're starting this writing journey too! You will be successful, I am sure of it! I can't wait until your series releases! I'm also proud of how strong a woman you are. We'll get to where we wanna be!!!

My WONDERFUL test readers! Jacole Coco Laryea, Michelle McQueen, and Novie Cuteeyez. Thank you, thank you, thank you for keeping me on my toes and ensuring I didn't drop some nonsense! Y'all were instrumental in my completing this book successfully. I would love to work with y'all again in the future! Thank you for staying by me despite my tardiness and indecisiveness. LOL

Thank you, Brittani Williams, for designing my wonderful cover! I love it! You always bring your A game whenever I hit you up. You're amazing!

To the readers—my loves—thank you for riding with me and purchasing this novel! You truly don't understand how much you mean to me. I love all of you. I hope you all like *Already Taken 2*.

Already TAKEN 2

Love N. Lee

Prologue

In 'Already Taken 1', Fallon reunited with her ex, a dope boy named Damontrez "Cash" Hardy. Their relationship ended originally due to Cash's street lifestyle. Now a year later, Fallon worried that things wouldn't work out seeing as he was still in the same line of work. To her surprise, he agreed to get out of the game for her and proposed shortly afterward.

Cash's younger brother, Delonte "Ghost" Hardy, had a bone to pick with him after being passed over as the next heir to Cash's drug empire. They got into it during Cash and Fallon's engagement party causing the bad blood between them to deepen. Problems arose for Cash and Fallon when they disagreed over how to handle the situation and she broke the engagement off.

Cash's other younger brother, Damien "Strap" Hardy, finally swept in and took this opportunity to confess his feelings for Fallon. He'd loved her since he was in high school, but she'd always brushed him off. Now that he'd matured, he hoped to get the woman he believed was always his. As the two reminisced on the past, he reminded Fallon of the night of passion they'd shared years ago and tried to convince her that he's the man for her…

Shantreis was fed up with her boyfriend Travaris "Outlaw" Robinson's doggish ways and decided to give him a taste of his own medicine when she started sleeping with Blaze, her ex from Virginia. Blaze wanted her to leave Outlaw, but she didn't want to give up her lavish lifestyle for one more modest with Blaze. When Outlaw started changing his ways and even proposed to Shantreis, she accepted, only to discover that she's pregnant and unsure of who the father is…

Meanwhile, Outlaw's baby's mother Kaleesha plotted on robbing him with her boyfriend Filthy. Unbeknownst to her, his cousin Blaze and Shantreis were also in on it. Shantreis had agreed to help Blaze so that he could make his own come up, but he also falsely believed she would be with him after he got the money. The robbery went without a hitch initially, but no one quite ended up with what they'd bargained for. Blaze got money, but not the girl. Filthy skipped town with Kaleesha's share of the money. After Outlaw learned that Kaleesha was behind it, he took their daughter Monet away from her.

Fallon reconciled with Cash, but after taking a bullet that was meant for him, she wanted to keep her distance. Unbeknownst to her, Ghost was the shooter, inspired to kill Cash after hearing Strap complain that they could have whatever they wanted if he was out of the picture. Cash placed a bounty on Ghost's head, while trying to get his woman back. To complicate things, Strap revealed to Cash that he wanted Fallon to himself. Strap was finally going to take what he felt was his. While Fallon was at home recovering, Strap went over to console her. The two ended up sleeping with one another. What they didn't count on was getting caught by a trigger-happy Cash...

Shantreis decided to leave Blaze alone and made up her mind that no matter what, Outlaw would be considered the father. Before she could even tell Outlaw of her pregnancy, he discovered a text message on her phone from Blaze, making him privy to the whole situation. Things quickly became physical, but Blaze arrived just in the nick of time. Shantreis was grateful but had mixed feelings after Blaze shot Outlaw then advised her to flee with Monet. With guilt on her shoulders and the police in her rearview mirror, she fears she made all the wrong decisions in life...

Chapter 1

"Damn, Strap... I always thought it was Ghost that wanted to be like me but you did too, huh? I understand that you love her. I really get that but the strength of the fact alone that she was—is," Cash corrected himself, "my girl—my fiancé, should've resolved that for you."

Cash shook his head and stared at Fallon thoughtfully. She was still knocked out. Seeing her lying underneath Strap in such a display of passion had him past heated and hurt. He couldn't explain how he felt at that moment but he was definitely in a dangerous place.

"I told you how I felt about her," Strap said sitting upright on the sofa, being sure to keep the sheet around him. "I couldn't cut that shit off, Cash. It may seem fucked up, but you would've done the same thing."

"Nope. That's where you're wrong. You should've voiced your feelings a long time ago!" Cash boomed. "You let the shit build up and get out of hand! All the women in this world that you could've chosen but you go after mine?!"

"They could never be Fallon."

"Nigga, I know that shit! But you could find a damned good replica!"

Fallon started to stir and rubbed her eyes slowly. "Cash?" she whispered.

A pained smile was on his face when she called his name, "It's fucked up, girl… I thought I was a good nigga. Whatever you *wanted* I did it for you… This is how you pay a nigga back?"

"Cash, I…" Fallon's voice cracked as she became overcome with emotion.

"Nah. I don't wanna hear that shit." Cash's voice sounded just as broken as hers did. His face even more so. He raised his gun and shook his head. "Death before dishonor is the code we abide by." His eyes were fixed on Fallon as he spoke before taking aim and pulling the trigger.

BLAOW!

"Shit!" Strap cursed as he dodged the bullet quickly, pulling Fallon down with him. *Was he aiming for me or Fallon?* he wondered. The two had been so close on the sofa that he couldn't really tell. *Maybe he didn't give a damn which one of us he hit…*

"Oh my God, Cash!" Fallon shrieked, finally finding her voice. "Are you crazy?"

Moving quickly, Strap reached for his jeans but he wasn't concerned about putting them on. He was looking for his trusty five pound.

"Stop!" Fallon cried hysterically when she saw Strap remove his gun and point it back at Cash. "Y'all are brothers!"

"Damn. You remember that now?" Cash asked sarcastically as he shook his head.

"Damontrez, let me explain," she started, although she honestly didn't know what to say. Still, Fallon thought it would be better than remaining silent.

"I'm good," Cash cut her off curtly, raising his hand. "Relax. If I wanted to kill y'all, I could've done it already. Believe that." He refocused his attention on Strap. "You can have her, nigga. A bitch like that ain't even worth it." Cash snickered to himself bitterly. He stood up and headed towards the front door. "Y'all deserve each other."

What have I done? Fallon wondered as she watched the door close behind him. *What should I do now?*

"Damn. That was fucked up," Strap mumbled to himself, taking a seat back on the sofa.

"Yeah," Fallon whispered, feeling like her heart was breaking. *If I feel this way, then I can only imagine how Cash feels... I have to go talk to him.*

Without a second thought, she hopped up and threw on her clothes.

"Fallon, where are you—?" Strap questioned, taking her hand as she tried to pass him. He was sure he already knew, but he couldn't stop himself from asking.

"I'll be back," she answered, breaking free of his grasp before dashing out the door. Taking the steps two at a time, Fallon nearly stumbled on the last step.

"Cash! Cash!" Fallon called, catching him right before he made it to his car. He ignored her, so she grabbed his arm. "Please, Damontrez... Just stop. Can I talk to you for a minute? Just one minute, please."

Grudgingly Cash paused, but he refused to make eye contact with her. His expression remained stone cold.

"I'm sorry... I'm so sorry!" she sobbed, clinging to his T-shirt like it was a lifeline. "If I could take it back I would! Please believe me!"

Why—because you got caught? Cash thought, but instead he asked, "You love him?"

Fallon opened her mouth to speak, but she didn't know what to say. An awkward silence washed over the two of them. "It's not like that," she admitted weakly. To be honest, she didn't exactly know *what* it was like but she wouldn't dare tell Cash that.

"Shit. If you don't love the nigga, that makes it worse," Cash replied, his voice void of any emotion. He refused to show Fallon how heartbroken he was. How disappointed he was. And most of all, how betrayed he felt. "Because then you could've chosen any nigga—*any* nigga would've been better than Strap... My baby brother... You chose to *fuck* my blood." His bitter laugh returned. "It's real fucked up."

Gently, he removed her grasp on his now soaked T-shirt. "Go back inside."

"So this is it, huh?" Fallon asked softly, seemingly in denial. "I guess you'll want this back then." She gazed pensively at her engagement ring before slipping it off her finger. "Here," she offered.

Cash shook his head. "Nah. You can keep it. I bought it for you, didn't I?"

A glimmer of hope flashed across her eyes. Could it be? "Really?" She started to put the ring back on but his next words made her pause.

"Yeah. It's just a piece of jewelry." Cash shrugged. "It's worthless now. It has no fuckin' meaning. Do whatever you want with it—throw it away, pawn it... I don't care." Turning his back to her, he continued to his car.

"Damontrez," Fallon begged futilely, but she didn't chase after him. What more was there to say? The damage had been done. Now all she could do was watch him walk out of her life.

"You straight?" Strap asked when Fallon reentered the apartment.

"Maybe you should go, too," she suggested numbly, ignoring his question. The pain from her wound was starting to hurt again. All she wanted to do was take her medication and sleep.

Strap nodded his head knowingly. He knew that Fallon still loved Cash, so he would give her space, but he hoped this wouldn't become another repeat of the past. No matter how many times she ran to him, it seemed she would always go back to Cash.

"You know I meant everything I said, right?" Strap offered, following her into her bedroom. "I always have."

"I don't think we'd work out," Fallon blurted as she sat on her bed. She slid her ring up and down her finger absently, staring at it intently. "I mean… I feel like I'm betraying Cash."

What? Strap looked at her in disbelief. It was a little late to feel that way wasn't it? The damage was done.

"Do you seriously think my brother would take you back after what just happened?" The question came out harsher than he'd intended. Hell, he hadn't even meant to say it but it rolled off his tongue before he could stop it.

"No… It's not about that. It's just… I'm not even really sure of my feelings," Fallon continued, "I was mad at Cash when… when all *this* happened. So I don't know if I even really meant it when I said 'I love you'."

"Damn," Strap uttered, not realizing he'd spoken aloud. The blow of her words hit him right in the heart—piercing him even deeper than Cash's bullet could have.

"Please try to understand the position I'm in."

"*You're* in?" he asked incredulously. "*I'm* in! That's my fuckin' brother. He's just a nigga to you!" Strap shook his head. "My flesh and blood! But I'm *still* willing to throw that away for you!"

"Maybe you shouldn't then," Fallon suggested quietly, averting her eyes from him.

"Where is this coming from? It's just cuz you feel guilty about my brother, right?" When she didn't respond, he continued, "I mean, we just said 'I love you' a couple of hours ago!"

"You don't really know much about me, Strap," she informed.

"I've known you for five years!" Strap protested.

Fallon shook her head. "Yeah. That's true, but you've only known what I've *shown* you, Damien. Do you really think you know everything about me just because we talked when I worked at Foot Action? How many times have we really interacted on a one-on-one level—discussing something more than me and Cash?" She focused her green eyes directly on Strap. "Don't forget that we were out of touch for about a year, too."

Strap was silent as he let her words sink in.

"I think you're just in love with who you *think* I am," she finished. "I *know* that's it."

"Nah," Strap spoke up finally. "It's not. What the hell do I have to do to prove it to you?"

"Did you know I got an abortion?"

"What?" His face contorted with confusion. "Why would I know that? Shit. Why would I even need to know that? You think I'm gonna—"

"If you really love me like you say you do, you have to be willing to accept all of me—the good *and* the bad."

"I mean…" Strap's voice trailed off. Her admission had taken him off guard. He wasn't a fan of abortions—in fact, he hated them. Still, how could he judge when he killed niggas for a living? Strap knew he didn't have a right. "It's the past… I'm sure you had your reasons for doing it."

"Would you still feel that way if it was yours?"

Strap's eyes narrowed. "Was it?"

Fallon nodded. "Yeah… It was," she admitted.

"W-what did you say?" Strap asked in shock. "Are you serious, Fallon? You were pregnant and didn't tell me—*and* you went and got an abortion? Why the fuck would you do that?" He felt himself trembling slightly with anger as his brain tried to process what she had just told him.

"You were eighteen, Strap! You couldn't take care of a baby! You were selling weed and living with your strung out mother! I was in college, doing internships and making the Dean's List. My parents are dead, who would've helped us?!" Her voice began to quiver, but she continued, "Who would've supported us? I know you couldn't possibly think that Cash would have!"

Strap was silent, trying hard to get a grip on his emotions before he lashed out on her. He'd always wanted to be a dad, especially since his own had been absent when he was growing up. The fact that Fallon took that honor away from him without his knowledge stung even more. He just needed to know one more thing.

"Did you feel bad about it?" he asked finally.

"What do you think?" Fallon said softly. "Of course I did. But I did what I had to do. If I had to do it all over again, I probably still would've done the same thing."

"You gotta be kiddin' me… We could've found a way!" Strap threw his hands up in frustration, pacing across the room angrily. "You don't think I would've changed if I knew?! I could've gotten a better job. Shit. I'd probably be a better nigga now if I had my seed." Strap shook his head sadly. "You don't understand what the fuck you did…"

"It was years ago, Damien," she pointed out. "I was with Cash, too. What would I have told him?"

"Man, you and that nigga broke up like what—a month after we fucked?" He waved her off. "Get out of here with that bullshit."

"Should I have just let him raise the baby as his?" she asked sarcastically, tired of being attacked. *I can't believe he's going in on me like this,* Fallon thought. *I know I did the right thing.*

"Is that seriously a question?"

"Yeah, it *is!*" Fallon shouted. "You know damn good and well if Cash had found out, *regardless* of whether or not we were broken up, both of our lives would be fucked up right now! Like I said, you were still living with your momma! Cash paid all *her* bills for y'all! I know you weren't making much from selling weed! You paid your car note and bought bullshit like the new Jordans and Girbauds, or whatever the hell niggas was wearing back then. You spent money the moment you got it!

"I would've had to drop out of school! You didn't go to college either, Strap, nor did you care about going at that time! Therefore you couldn't have done shit but get a job at McDonald's making minimum wage! How the hell can you take of a child like that?! I wasn't about to become another statistic living off the system just because you selfishly wanted me to keep a child we couldn't afford!"

"Bi—" Strap had to resist the urge to call her a bitch. It almost slipped from his mouth, but he was glad he refrained. "You don't know what the fuck I would've done if I had known! If it meant providing my child with a better life, you don't think I'd do whatever the fuck I had to do?!"

"Okay. So what you're saying is that you would've gone to school?" She didn't give him a chance to respond before continuing, "Let's go with that scenario then. School takes at least two to four years to complete, Damien. It's not an overnight thing. You'd need a job while you're going to school so you *still* would've been making minimum wage. How would you afford school? Not just that, but who says you would've even got a job at the end of the day?"

"I know that shit, Fallon! You contradictin' ya damn self! If you ain't think I would a' got a job anyway then why bring up that I ain't got a college education?! I know the shit ain't guaranteed! Look at the fuckin' economy! I never said I was gonna go to school. I just said I'd do whatever!"

Fallon rolled her eyes. "So what? You were gonna continue to sell drugs, I guess, and then end up locked up?" She clapped her hands condescendingly. "Great choice. Just what the world needs—another black man in jail and another child without a father in his life."

"You sound stupid as hell right now!" Strap yelled. "That was shit I *was* doing! Not what I *would've* been doing! Hell, I could've gotten a job working at ACS. Niggas working there was makin' decent money."

"That's in Raleigh, Strap. You would've had to move to Greensboro."

"So fuckin' what? It's jobs there!"

"You're also forgetting I couldn't afford to go to college without Cash. I wouldn't have had any money to stay off-campus. I can't live at the dorm with a baby! Let's not forget that *Cash* bought my BMW and he probably would've taken that shit away." Strap opened his mouth to speak, but she continued, "Even if he would've let me keep it, I wouldn't have been able to pay that high ass insurance or fill that gas guzzler up all the time!"

"You negative as fuck. You just wanna *believe* the shit would've been all bad cuz you feel guilty! You know what you did was fucked up! Damn! You pregnant for nine months, Fallon. By the time you had the baby, I would've had a good ass job and been able to upgrade us to a two bedroom apartment. Greensboro is cheaper than Raleigh any damn way. I'm sure you had a homegirl you could've stayed with until I got us a place. But honestly, while you talkin' out the side of ya neck and shit, I know Cash paid your rent upfront so you would a' *still* had a place to stay. The shit was in your name!

"As far as school goes, you could've taken out a loan! Plenty of college kids can't afford the shit either! If everybody had to pay out they pocket, it would be a lot of uneducated muthafuckas in the world! You had one damn semester left! Ain't no way you'd have to borrow that much damn money for that! We would've been alright."

"Whatever, Strap! I'm done!" Fallon threw her hands up in annoyance. "You just refuse to hear what I'm saying!"

"You right. I don't give a fuck about what you sayin' cuz it's bullshit!"

"No. It's called being realistic! Maybe you only see it positively because you're young." She shrugged her shoulders. "I don't know what it is."

"Because I'm young?" he repeated incredulously. "The fuck? Don't treat me like these other lil' niggas runnin' around Raleigh! You know I ain't shit like them. That's why you fucked with me in the first place."

"We *fucked*, Strap. That was it. I could've been with you but we both know how the story ends—I ended up with Cash."

Fallon was so angry, that she didn't care—or possibly even notice—how hurtful her words were. Her defense mechanism had kicked in. Whenever she felt like someone was attacking her, she would strike back even harder to make herself feel better.

"Oh yeah? Damn. It's like that?" Strap asked in disbelief. He nodded his head. "You was right. I don't know you. I don't know who the fuck this chick is sitting in front of me."

The pitiful expression on Strap's face tugged at her heartstrings. Quickly she found herself softening her tone, "Damien, I'm human, too! I make mistakes! You hold me up on this ridiculously high pedestal! I just wanted—"

"Yeah. You right. You just fell all the way off that shit!" Strap interjected. "You could've been told me this shit, Fallon! Hell, to keep it real with you, I wish you would've never said shit about it in the first place!"

"So you wanted me to lie to you?!"

Strap shot her a piercing look. "You know what I mean, Fallon! I bet you never told my brother we fucked back then and I'm sure you'll never tell him, right?"

"No. Why would I?"

"Exactly my point. So you ain't had to tell me this shit either."

"If I knew you would act like this then I wouldn't have! But I think this shows I was right! You don't know me and you obviously never loved me—not like you thought!"

Strap shook his head as he turned to walk out of the room, not bothering to dignify her with a response. *Maybe she's right...* He definitely still had *feelings* for her, but now he wasn't quick to call it love.

Strap paused at the doorway. "Can you answer this question for me right quick, though?"

"What is it?" she asked nearly inaudibly.

"If the baby had been my brother's, would you have aborted it then, too?"

An uncomfortable silence fell between them for two minutes, with Strap searching her eyes for the truth. Finally, she responded, "No, I wouldn't have, okay? You happy now? Cash would've been able to take care of—"

Strap raised his hand, signaling for her to stop. "That's what I thought. That's all I needed to hear."

Chapter 2

I can't believe that fuckin' bitch! Outlaw thought. He clenched his fists angrily as he paced back and forth around the bedroom. *She really wouldn't have told me shit if I ain't seen that damn text message! I swear I wanna kill that bitch!*

He looked back at Shantreis with rage in his eyes. He'd choked her for so long she'd blacked out. Outlaw would've kept on until she took her last breath if Monet hadn't come up the stairs and saw him. She had still been talking about the damn FedEx man at the door. *That's the only reason why you're still alive, bitch...*

"Shan-shan! Shan-shan, wake up!" Monet sobbed, shaking her softly.

"Get out, Monet!"

Monet gave Shantreis one last fleeting glance before doing as she was told, but stopped in the doorway to ask one last question, "Are you sure she's okay?"

"Monet, go in the other room now or I'm a' whup your ass!" he barked.

As soon as she left, Outlaw slammed the door behind her and refocused his attention on Shantreis. Every time he looked at her, he grew even more incensed. It didn't help that he'd overheard her mumbling Blaze's name a few times. *She dreaming about this nigga too? Hell nah!*

"Scandalous ass bitch!" Outlaw roared. He picked up a lamp from the nightstand and hurled it at the wall.

CRASH!

Shantreis stirred softly from the commotion and opened her eyes slightly. Her vision was blurry but she could hear just fine. It was definitely Outlaw's voice she was hearing. *But... I was on 540 and the police were after me,* she thought in confusion, but it didn't take long for her to put two and two together. *Oh no... None of that was real? I just passed out?* Once the realization washed over her, she just wanted to cry out in defeat.

She was terrified.

Outlaw didn't have a problem with killing anyone. He'd certainly killed for less than this. He actually *loved* her, so Shantreis could only imagine what would happen to her now. Her fate would be much worse than that of a stranger. She was sure of it.

How the hell am I gonna get out of this now? There's no way that Blaze is gonna come rescue me like he did in my dream... Shantreis blinked back her tears, trying to regain her composure so Outlaw wouldn't notice she'd awoken.

"After this same shit happened with Kaleesha, I still went and wifed up another ho! Bitches ain't worth shit!" Outlaw ranted as he continued to break anything within his reach.

Lord, she prayed silently... desperately... urgently... If He couldn't help her, then who could? Shantreis squeezed her eyes tightly and clasped her hands together. *You know I never ask you for anything, right? So please, please help me get out of this alive! I swear I will be so thankful! I'll even start going to church sometimes! Just please don't let him kill me! You know I don't deserve this! I just made a mistake! Please! In Jesus' name I pray, amen!*

Cautiously she opened her eyes, only to find Outlaw hovering over her.

"Why the fuck you still layin' there if you awake?!" Yanking her by the ankle, he slid her across the bed until she landed in a heap on the floor. "Get the fuck outta my house!" he bellowed, smacking her upside the head for emphasis. "Stupid ass."

Shantreis's first instinct was to hit him, but considering the situation, she knew that wouldn't be the smartest move. Her body was aching and sore from how roughly her bottom had hit the floor, but she ignored the pain. Instead she stood up calmly. *If I listen to his bitch ass maybe he'll leave me alone.* Shantreis walked to the bathroom to put her maxi dress back on and stared at her reflection in the mirror. Her hair was a tangled mess. Her eyes were slightly red and watery from crying.

I wish Blaze really did come get me, she thought. *I felt bad when that nigga shot him in my dream, but now I wish that shit was real.*

"Bitch, I proposed to yo' triflin' ass! I changed for you and this is what you do?" she could hear Outlaw shouting. With just a quick glimpse, Shantreis saw he was close to destroying their lavish master bedroom. "You fuck around with that pussy ass nigga?!!"

After straightening her hair, she made her way out of the bathroom slowly, being careful to avoid him. *I just wanna get my shit and leave before this psycho ass nigga tries to put his hands on me again.* As she headed to the closet to begin packing her things, Outlaw's loud, condescending voice stopped her mid-step.

"Nah, bitch, you ain't takin' none of that shit with you! Anything I bought with my fuckin' money is mine!"

Shantreis scowled as she turned around to face him. "You a petty ass muthafucka, Outlaw! You got all this fuckin' money and you can't let me have my shit?!" she questioned incredulously. Although she hated crying, she couldn't stop the tears that sprung to her eyes.

"Tell that nigga to replace the shit then!" he shouted. "You lucky I'm *lettin'* you have your life. Be thankful, bitch!"

Shantreis wiped at her tears, hating how pitiful she probably looked. *I can't believe this nigga! What the fuck is he gonna do with my shit anyway? Give it to some other bitch?*

Outlaw snapped his fingers as if remembering something. "Oh yeah. One more thing." He stalked towards her with his fists balled. Unconsciously, her hands went to protect her stomach.

"Don't worry, bitch, I ain't gonna beat that baby out of you! I should though."

"I told you it's your baby, Outlaw."

"Bitch, shut the fuck up with your lyin' ass!" he demanded, smacking her in the mouth and instantly busting her lip. "Yo' hoe ass probably don't even know who your fuckin' baby daddy is. But even if it *is* mine, I don't want shit to do with it!"

"We don't want shit to do with you either, nigga," Shantreis snapped back with an attitude.

Fuck that. I'm tired of this shit! I'll be damned if I'm gonna sit here and let him talk to me any kind of way. Shit. This ain't his first time going through this, she thought, realizing how she and

Kaleesha's situation now echoed one another. *Except she knew that Monet was Outlaw's... I didn't before, but now I hope this is Blaze's baby.*

Outlaw turned his attention to her left hand. "Take my fuckin' ring off. You don't deserve that shit!" He yanked the diamond engagement ring off her finger, nearly breaking it off. "Now get—"

The sound of her phone ringing interrupted his statement. He pulled it out of his pocket and read the Caller ID. Fallon's name was on the display but Outlaw knew better. "Fuck that nigga!" Violently he flung the phone at Shantreis, smacking her in the face.

"Daddy! Come quick! Hurry, hurry! I want this!" Monet yelled from downstairs.

"Daddy's busy right now, Monet!"

"Please, Daddy! Come here! You're gonna miss it!"

Outlaw sighed in annoyance, but followed his daughter's request. "Ay, be gone by the time I come back up here," he warned.

"I will." Shantreis waited a couple of seconds after Outlaw left before answering the phone. She didn't even bother with the pleasantries. "I can't believe your stupid ass! This is all your fuckin' fault! I'm losing everything because of your dumb ass."

"Hello?" Blaze asked, unsure as to whether Shantreis was talking to him or entertaining another conversation in the background. "Ay, what's going on? You need me to come get you?"

"No! Fuck you, Blaze!" she shrieked. She rushed to grab her purse. It was another item she was sure Outlaw didn't want her to have, but fuck it. As long as she hurried out he wouldn't even know. *My keys are still in here and I got a couple of my credit cards…*

"Are you serious right now, Shantreis? Whatever happened is your own damn fault!" Blaze's voice boomed from the phone receiver. "If you weren't so money hungry, fuckin' with a nigga like him! If you was mine, you wouldn't have shit to worry about!"

"No! Are *you* serious?" Shantreis countered hysterically. "If I was yours, I wouldn't *have* shit! You broke as fuck!"

"It's always about money with you, ain't it? You'd rather stay with a nigga with money that beats your ass than be with a good nigga with a stable job!"

"Yeah! It is!" she admitted without shame. "I grew up broke! I'm not going back to that!"

"Looks like you ain't got a choice now, huh?" Blaze asked sarcastically.

He was still talking, but Shantreis was no longer listening. She had refocused her attention on the doorway where Outlaw now stood.

"You still here?" he asked. His patience was wearing thin. The longer Shantreis stayed in his presence, the angrier he became.

"I'm going!" she shrieked.

"Who you on the phone with?" Outlaw asked suddenly. "That pussy ass nigga? In *my* fuckin' house?" He snatched the phone out of her hand then hurled it at their mirror, shattering it instantly.

"Really, Travaris?" Shantreis muttered as she went to retrieve her broken phone. The screen was cracked and black. It was safe to say it was probably inoperable.

If I don't have a phone, then who the fuck is gonna come get me? I know his punk ass ain't gonna let me take my Jag. Desperately, she pressed the power button, willing it to come on.

"Hurry up and get yo' ass out!" Outlaw jerked her by the arm, pulling her along roughly, but Shantreis tugged back.

"Don't put your hands on me, nigga!" she warned. "I can walk my damn self!"

"What the fuck you gonna do, bitch?" he taunted, striking her face with his fist brutally. He looked at her with a smug expression, daring her to fight back.

"If you put your hands on me again, I'll call the police on your simple ass!!!" she threatened, clutching her face in pain.

Outlaw stood there in shock. *Did this bitch--?*

"What the fuck did you just say?" he demanded as rage overcame him. Spittle flew from his mouth in anger. Without giving her a chance to reply, Outlaw raised his foot and kicked her in the stomach callously. "I swear to fuckin' God!" He stared at her menacingly, watching her crumple to the floor in pain.

"Oh God!" Shantreis cried in agony. She curled into a fetal position. She placed her hands between her legs in a weak attempt to stop the bleeding that was dying her white maxi dress a bright red.

"Bitch, if you ever threaten my muthafuckin' livelihood again, I swear I will kill your ass!" Outlaw was so far gone that he didn't even realize what he had done, nor did he feel any remorse. He knelt down next to her and grabbed her throat to emphasize his point. "You know how the fuck I get down! Muthafuckas won't ever find your body! Understand?"

Shantreis nodded her head weakly.

"Now get ya ass up!" he hollered. Gruffly, Outlaw pulled her to her feet. Shantreis held onto him for support as he roughly escorted her down the stairs and towards the front door.

"Shan-shan, where are you going?" Monet asked from the sofa, but her question went ignored.

"If you told that nigga to come get you, don't bring his bitchass in front of my fuckin' house," Outlaw warned as he pushed her outside, nearly causing her to slip on the FedEx envelope left on the porch. "I'll kill both of y'all. Don't sit in my fuckin' yard either!" With those last words, he slammed the door.

Shantreis walked hunched over with one hand between her legs and the other clutching her stomach. She felt lightheaded. She wanted nothing more than to sit down but she wanted to get as far away from Outlaw as possible.

My fuckin' life is a mess. I'm homeless, pregnant, and alone, Shantreis thought miserably as she trudged down the walkway barefoot. *What's going to happen to me?*

A sudden jolt of pain shot through her belly, causing her to cry out. "Agghh! I-I need help…" were the last words to escape her lips before she collapsed into the street.

Chapter 3

I can't believe Fallon actually did that shit! Hell, I can't believe she even told me that shit! What the fuck was she thinkin'? Strap thought, lifting a Newport cigarette to his lips and inhaling the menthol. Smoking cigarettes was something he'd never cared for, but this evening he found himself buying a pack from Han-Dee Hugo's.

"They keep tellin' me 'don't save you'. If I ignore all that advice and something isn't right then who will I complain to?" Drake crooned from the speakers of his car.

"The real her," Strap scoffed, thinking about the irony between the song playing and what Fallon had shown him. He leaned back against the hood of his Charger and blew the smoke from his nostrils. He was outside of Triangle Town Center Mall waiting for his brother to show up. He was running late, but Strap wasn't complaining. He had plenty of other things on his mind.

"I done fucked up my relationship with my brother, for what? A sneaky ass female I ain't even sure if I want any—" Before Strap could finish his statement, he felt the barrel of a gun press against the back of his head.

"Nigga, quit bitchin' and gimme ya fuckin' money!"

Strap raised his hands hoping not to provoke the robber, but gave him a warning, "Nigga, trust me, this ain't some shit you wanna do. You got the wrong muthafuckin' one!"

"Blaow!" a familiar obnoxious voice cried out. "Caught ya ass slippin'!"

"Nigga, you play too fuckin' much!" Strap frowned as he looked at his twin brother.

Ghost was dressed in his usual attire—jeans that sagged off his waist, the latest pair of Jordans, and a black, oversized hoodie. The hood covered his head, but Strap knew he'd cut off his signature dreads before heading down to Jacksonville in an attempt to disguise himself... At least, Strap thought that was the real reason. Let Ghost tell it, he was just tired of getting them re-twisted.

Ghost laughed as he tucked his gun back into his pants. "Whassup, Strap?" He held his hand out for a shake, and the two men hugged.

"Too much shit... But I can't believe you brought yo' ass back to Raleigh. You bolder than a muthafucka."

Ghost shrugged. "You think I'm a' just let a muh'fucka kick me out of my fuckin' city? Heeelll nah. I told you my ol' lady's grandma died so I went with her." He narrowed his eyes at Strap. "Fuck you thought—a nigga was scared?!"

Now it was Strap's turn to shrug. He took another pull of the cigarette. He was sure Ghost was just trying to save face, but he wasn't in the mood to call him out on it. Then again, knowing how unpredictable and reckless Ghost could be at times, it was a very real possibility.

"What the hell you out here talkin' 'bout?" Ghost asked, taking a seat on the hood of his car.

"Man…" Strap shook his head. "Got damn Fallon…"

"Damn, nigga, it's like that?" Ghost chuckled, "Bitch got you smokin' Newports and shit." He frowned. "Nigga, is you listenin' to Drake?! Soft ass nigga!"

"Man, shut the fuck up." Strap chuckled. "But hell yeah… Cash caught me and Fallon this morning—"

"Fuck you mean 'caught'? Y'all fucked or some shit?" Strap nodded in confirmation. "Damn. Where y'all was at?"

Strap took a deep breath before filling his brother in with all the pertinent details.

"Damn," Ghost repeated after Strap finished. "Cash better than me cuz I would a' murked both y'all asses! Ay, I know you love that bitch or whatever, but she scandalous. Fuck that bitch, for real."

Strap sighed. "I'm mad as hell, but I think I still love her. I ain't even gonna lie to you. That shit was just fucked up though. She aborted my seed and I swear…"

"Fuck her," Ghost reiterated. "It's plenty pussy out here. Matter fact, look at that bitch over there." He pointed to a short, dark-skinned beauty with her hair cut into a stylish bob. "She works with my ol' lady. She bad but she stuck up. You might could get her though."

"The last thing I wanna be bothered with is another female," Strap confessed, but he had to admit the girl was cute. She had big brown eyes framed by long lashes and a slim but curvy shape.

"Ay, Taeja!" Ghost shouted, ignoring his brother. "Tae, lemme holla at you for a second!"

Taeja looked in their direction and rolled her eyes. "What do you want, D? Malaysia's coming out in a minute."

He sucked his teeth at the mention of his girlfriend. "What's that supposed to mean?"

"That means quit trying to talk to me when you're spoken for already. I told you I'm not interested. A street nigga doesn't have shit to offer me," she replied.

"Get the fuck outta here with that shit." Ghost turned to Strap. "That bitch bourgeois as fuck, ain't she? But shit, that's yo' type, ain't it?"

Here we go again, Strap thought to himself, having momentarily forgotten how outspoken and tactless Ghost could be.

"Ay, chill the fuck out. Shawty was mindin' her own business." Strap looked over at Taeja, who had posted up behind an older model Toyota with her arms folded.

Before Ghost could reply, a voice called out in their direction, "Bae! I need a favor!"

Approaching them was a brown skinned girl. She wore a long, blonde Nicki Minaj inspired weave in her head. As she spoke, the gold bottom grill in her mouth shined against the lighting in the mall's parking lot. Without even having to be introduced, Strap knew this was Malaysia—but in case he was unsure, her name was tattooed on the side of her neck.

She's definitely Ghost's type, Strap thought. *Hood as fuck.* He remembered her faintly as the chick Ghost had kept on the side when he was dealing with Ri-Ri. They had all smoked together a few times but that was the extent of his contact with her.

"Man, hell nah," Ghost said. "What is it?"

Malaysia nodded in the direction of Taeja, who was now walking towards them. "I told Tae we could give her a ride home since her car fucked up. That's cool, right?"

Ghost eyed Taeja. "You got gas money?"

"Are you serious right now?" Taeja asked. She only had a couple of dollars in her pocket and needed every cent of it.

"I'm dead ass! Shit. Gas 'bout $5 a fuckin' gallon. You think I'm 'bout to chauffeur yo' ass for free? Where you stay?"

"The Oaks at Brier Creek."

"Exactly. Too fuckin' far."

"Baby, she don't have—" Malaysia started, but Strap cut her off.

"I can take you. I don't mind."

Taeja studied him carefully before shaking her head. "Thanks, but no thanks. I don't really know you like that."

"What you think he gonna kidnap you or some shit?" Ghost cut in.

"He's a good nigga," Malaysia tried to assure her. "Besides, I know you ain't got no other ride. Won't the babysitter charge you extra if you pick up Kairi late?"

Taeja sighed, knowing her friend was right. "Well…"

"Trust me. He's cool."

Strap put out his cigarette, then held out his hand in an attempt to convince her, "I'm Damien."

"I'm Taeja," she replied politely. Their eyes met briefly before she placed her hand in his. "Nice to meet you."

"Likewise." He made his way over to the passenger door, holding it open for her.

Ghost sucked his teeth. "This nigga here. Ay, after you drop her off then stop by the crib."

"A'ight," Strap agreed before getting inside of his car and starting the engine.

"Thank you for offering to give me a ride," Taeja said nervously as she buckled her seatbelt. "That was really nice of you."

"No problem."

Taeja looked around his car, admiring how clean it was. As they pulled out of the parking lot, she stole a few glances at him, trying to memorize his face in case something happened. At least that was what she tried to convince herself. *He's really good looking and clean cut. I like the way he dresses.*

"You said you stay around Brier Creek, right?" Strap asked, breaking her from her thoughts.

"Yes."

Strap nodded his head. *I just left from over there,* he thought. Fallon stayed five minutes away from Taeja.

I don't wanna give you the wrong impression... I need love and affection...

Hearing his phone go off and recognizing Fallon's ringtone, Strap quickly pressed 'Ignore'. *Why the hell is she callin' me?*

"I won't get you in trouble with your girl, right?" Taeja asked seriously.

"Huh? How you figure I got a girl?"

"Just asking. You look like you would... And I'm sure that ringtone isn't for one of your niggas," she joked.

Strap cracked a smile at her assessment. "You right, but nah, she ain't my girl no more. She did some dumb shit and fucked it up."

"Well, maybe y'all can work it out."

"Hell nah." He shook his head. "She *just* told me that two years ago she aborted my baby! Then she kept makin' excuses for why she did the shit. I don't know how the fuck I'm supposed to feel…"

"Wow…" she near whispered. "I'm sorry to hear that."

"It's some more shit but I ain't tryna get into all that," Strap answered, hoping she wouldn't ask any more questions. Honestly, he didn't know why he'd told her in the first place. *I just met this girl and I'm telling her my business.*

"Well, you love her, right?"

"I guess…" His voice trailed off as he thought about what Fallon said to him earlier. "I thought I did, but now I don't know."

"If you could fall out of love that quickly over something like that, then maybe it wasn't really love. But if you do really love her, then you should forgive her. She told you for a reason, right?" Taeja suggested. "It was probably really bothering her and she felt guilty about holding it in. I bet it was really hard for her, too."

Strap was silent as he pondered Taeja's words. On one hand he felt she was right, but it still didn't change how hurt he felt.

Her opinion would probably change if she knew the only reason she aborted it was because it was my *baby.* Truth be told, it was more than just her aborting the baby that hurt Strap. It was everything else she'd said. *Females always know the right fuckin' buttons to press.*

"My bad," Taeja apologized, feeling like she'd overstepped her bounds.

"Huh?" Strap shook his head as he merged onto I-540 W. "Nah. You straight. I just got a lot of shit on my mind."

Taeja nodded in understanding and turned her attention back outside the window. The rest of the ride was pretty quiet until they got closer to Brier Creek.

"And just make a left right here," Taeja instructed before pointing at an apartment building. "You can just let me out here."

Strap followed her directions and pulled into a parking space.

"Thanks again for the ride." She smiled. "I really appreciate it. I swear I'll pay you back."

"Nah. You good. I ain't like my brother." Strap chuckled. "Let me know you got in safe."

"It's actually my babysitter's building. I stay over there." Taeja motioned to a couple of buildings away.

"Oh shit. I can drive you over there," he offered. "If yo' baby daddy ain't gonna trip, that is."

"Really?" Her face brightened, showing off her two deep dimples. "And no, there's no baby daddy in the picture. Thank you. I'll be right back."

Strap admired her retreating figure with a smile, wondering if what Ghost said was right. A new female could probably take his mind off Fallon.

When he saw her approaching the car with a baby's car seat in hand and a huge baby bag hanging from her other shoulder, he quickly exited the car to help her. "I got you."

"I'm good. I'm used to it."

"Nah," Strap insisted as he took the handle from her, alleviating her from the heavy car seat. He peered down at the little girl sitting inside of it. She looked to be maybe seven or eight months old with a head full of curly, dark brown hair. Big round green eyes peered back at him, immediately making him think about Fallon.

Is this what our daughter would've looked like? he wondered. "What's your daughter's name?"

"Her name's Kairi, but she's not my daughter," Taeja replied, taking the car seat from Strap as they drew closer to the car.

While she secured Kairi in the backseat, she explained her situation. "She's actually my niece. After my sister and her baby's father died, I stood up and took custody of her so she wouldn't go to foster care. My Grandma wanted to take her in, but she's too old and wheelchair-bound now. I've had to change my lifestyle since having her in my life, but it's worth it."

"Damn…" Strap uttered, nodding his head in agreement. "That's real big of you, Taeja."

"Yeah. I'm doing it on my own. I feel like a single mother." She laughed. "It's hard sometimes. I graduated from college a couple of months ago but I still haven't been able to get a job in my major yet. I just moved back to Raleigh from Greensboro after my sister died, too. So for now I'm working at Victoria's Secret until a better opportunity comes up."

Strap was sure he'd never met a female like her before. "Well, if you ever—" Before he could finish his statement, his phone vibrated, alerting him of a new text message.

When he noticed Fallon was the sender, he was tempted not to open it but curiosity got the best of him. After all, what the hell else could she possibly have to say that hadn't been said already?

I'm so sorry about earlier… Believe me. I really do love you and I need you right now. Please forgive me.

Fuck, Strap thought. He stared at the screen for a few seconds before typing 'I'm on my way'. *Nah… Hell nah.*

Deleting the message, he placed his phone back into his pocket.

Chapter 4

I'm so sorry about earlier... Believe me. I really do love you and I need you right now. Please forgive me.

Cash looked down at the text message from Fallon again as he stood in front of the door awaiting entry. *How the fuck could she send me some shit like that... after what she did?*

Fallon's earlier apologies echoed in his head. Each time he thought about it, he grew angrier. *I probably need to take my black ass back home,* Cash thought. *Before I end up doin' some shit I'm a' regret...* That's what he told himself but his feet were planted firmly on her welcome mat. *Man, fuck it.*

Cash had downed a couple of shots before coming over so he attributed his brash decision on that. His reasoning was twisted, but this was going to be Fallon's punishment... whether she knew it or not.

"Cash?" she asked as she opened her front door. "What are you—?"

He cut off her questioning by covering her lips with his, effectively swallowing her words. There wasn't shit to say, and if there was, he wasn't in the mood to explain himself. Pushing himself inside of her apartment, he kicked the door shut behind him before pressing her against the wall.

Cash slid up her Victoria's Secret satin slip, pleased to find she wasn't wearing any panties. Quickly unbuckling his pants, he pulled out his manhood and parted her legs, maneuvering his body to fill the space between her legs. He cupped her butt cheeks, lifting her small frame off the ground.

"Oh Lord," she gasped as he split her walls, bouncing her up and down on his thickness with force. He moved her quickly and roughly. For a second, she thought she would break in half.

Cash walked down the hallway towards her bedroom, never losing his pace. After placing her on the bed, he flipped her over doggy style and continued where he'd left off. The overpowering desire to hurt her entered his mind. Each thrust he gave became more brutal. Envisioning Fallon with Strap only fueled Cash's anger. Hearing her cries of passion made it worse.

Was she like this with him? Cash wondered. *What the fuck was she thinking?* Consumed with a wild combination of hate, passion, love, and lust, he took it all out on her.

"Cash, you're hurting me," she whined, but Cash didn't ease up until five minutes later when he pulled out, spilling his seed onto her backside.

"You for-forgive me?" she managed, placing her hands between her legs to ease the soreness she felt. When she didn't receive an answer, she went to the bathroom to clean herself off.

Cash laid back on the bed, well-spent after the workout he'd given her. Yet somehow he still didn't feel content.

Hearing his phone vibrate again, he picked it up although he already knew who it was. Hell, Fallon had been blowing up his phone all night.

"What's going on with you and Fallon?" she asked as she reentered the room.

Cash hit the 'Ignore' button as he looked up. "I don't wanna talk about that shit, Remy. If I came to see you, then do you think I wanna talk about another bitch? That's your damn problem—you always worried about shit that ain't got nothin' to do with you." He powered off his phone before placing it back in his pocket.

Remy narrowed her hazel eyes as she lifted his head and positioned it on top of her honey-colored thighs. "Nigga, you just came in my house, punished *my* pussy *probably* because of that bitch, and you don't wanna talk about it?" She tossed her long, Peruvian weave over her shoulder.

Cash sighed, figuring she was somewhat right. "Shit's dead. She fucked up. That's the end of it."

"Really?" Remy laughed bitterly. "That's funny. Sounds a lot like what you said last time and look what you fucked around and did! You ended up proposing to that bitch."

He only shrugged in response, not in the mood for where Remy was trying to take the conversation.

"I don't know what the hell happened between y'all but maybe this time you'll really leave that bitch alone." She ran her fingers through his dreads gently. "Is that the only reason why you came here... for some pussy?"

Cash closed his eyes, enjoying the scalp massage he was receiving. "To be honest, I don't really know why the hell I came over here. I said I wasn't gonna fuck with yo' ass no more."

"You *always* say that but you never mean it. Look at what happened last time." She smiled. "You must've missed me."

Cash looked up at the tattoo of his name inked in cursive script on her left breast. 'Damontrez Hardy'. She'd gotten it a few years back in an attempt to show him she could be his 'ride or die' chick. Remy had always been loyal to him for reasons he couldn't begin to understand. No matter how many times he put her second, she constantly put him first.

"Yeah. You right," he admitted.

"Really?" Remy asked with surprise, beaming even wider than before. She couldn't tell if he was humoring her or not, but it still made her feel good. "I missed you, too."

"I really can't believe that bitch ass nigga," Shantreis said, her body trembling and shaking. She had been repeating the same words over and over to herself. She was still in disbelief.

Shantreis was currently sitting in a hospital bed at WakeMed. A neighbor had discovered her passed out in the street and wasted no time calling for help.

"Because of that nigga, I could've fuckin' died!" she shouted angrily. "Outlaw, your ass is bitch made!"

"Shantreis! What happened?" Fallon shrieked as she entered the room, not even bothering to knock. Before Shantreis could reply, her friend had even more questions. "What happened to your face? Oh my God…" She reached down to hug her friend before reexamining her face. "You look…"

"Horrible. I know," Shantreis filled in the blank.

"Where's Outlaw at?" Fallon asked, unaware of the full situation. When Shantreis called, the only thing she'd told her was that she was in the hospital and requested a change of clothes. She'd failed to mention the circumstances behind it. Fallon had been in her own funk, but she brushed it off for the sake of her friend.

"Are you okay? Is..." Fallon lowered her tone as though they weren't the only two in the room. "Is the baby okay?"

Shantreis shook her head slowly before breaking down into tears. "That muthafucka... That muthafucka nearly killed my..."

Fallon's eyes widened in shock. "Not the baby! O-Outlaw? Why? Did he--?" She clamped her hands over her mouth. "He found out?"

Shantreis nodded.

"How? Oh my God!" she exclaimed. "He's a monster! Did you tell the police?"

Shantreis screwed her face up, wiping her tears away. "Hell no. And I'm *not* gonna tell them either."

Fallon rolled her eyes. "Why? Because of that 'no snitching' bullshit? Or are you trying to protect him?"

"Protect him?" she asked incredulously. "Are you crazy? Why the fuck would I do that? Did you not hear what he did to me?! Do you not see it?!" Her hands shook in anger. "I'm gonna deal with it myself."

"What can you do, Shantreis? You're just gonna do something stupid and get arrested for it? It's not worth it."

"So what—You want me to call the law like they're really gonna believe me when I say he did it? Be for real. What evidence do I have? He's got the money for a good ass lawyer and I ain't got shit." Outlaw's departing words to her echoed in her head again: *"Bitch, if you ever threaten my muthafuckin' livelihood again, I swear I will kill your ass!"* Shantreis believed it without a doubt, but she would find her own way to deal with him.

"Just forget about it, Fallon. I got shit under control."

"I hope so," Fallon said doubtfully, before changing the subject. "Did you tell Blaze yet?"

"Fuck him!" Shantreis spat. "It's all his fault anyway!" Blaze had been calling her persistently but all thirty of his calls went unanswered. She didn't even bother to listen to the voicemails he'd left.

"You need to tell him, Treis," Fallon's tone softened. "It's a chance that it's his baby. He needs to know."

"Outlaw wouldn't let me take shit," she changed the subject. Shantreis was still undecided about whether or not she wanted to deal with Blaze. There were much more important things on her mind. "So I was wondering if I could stay at your house until I..." Her voice faltered.

Until I do what—get a job? Shantreis thought bitterly. *The last time I had a job was when I was eighteen before I met that muthafucka. I ain't go to college... Who the fuck will hire me? Burger King?*

"That's fine," Fallon assured her, breaking Shantreis from her dismal thoughts.

"Fallon, what the fuck am I gonna do?" Shantreis cried. "I can't live at your house for the rest of my fuckin' life!"

"Well, maybe Blaze will give you some money to help you out. After all, you helped him get it."

Shantreis nodded. "You right. That nigga owes me. It's the least he could do. I know he ain't blow all that in three weeks."

Fallon smiled. "Good. That should make you feel a little better."

"Yeah," she sniffed. "I'm a' be straight. I'm just real pissed about how Outlaw tried me... That nigga actually did some shit like this without even caring that it could a' been his child!" Unconsciously she found her voice rising. "The doctor says I gotta be on modified bedrest if I wanna carry the baby to term... But you know what?"

Shantreis paused. "I really thought I had lost my baby... I started to think that maybe that would've been a good thing. You know?" Tears once again pooled in her eyes and rolled down her cheeks. "I probably won't be a good mom anyway."

"Shantreis," Fallon said quietly, covering her mouth with her hand. "Don't say that."

"Hell, I was talking about getting rid of it before." Choked up from her tears, she finally released a loud sob. Fallon took a seat on the bed and embraced her friend. "But you know what, Fallon? I was just so damn scared. It was then that I really *really* wanted my baby. I really t-thought that it was going to be ta-ta-taken away from me!"

"It's gonna be okay," she consoled her friend. "You have your baby and you have a second chance at it." As Fallon held Shantreis, her own problems seemed so trivial at the moment. She realized she could've been in the same exact predicament.

Shantreis wiped her runny nose and nodded her head with conviction. "Yeah. It's not okay yet, but it will be. I'll get that nigga back. Just like he tried to take away my child, I'll take his so he can feel exactly like I did."

"Don't say that... You don't mean that."

"Yes the hell I do, Fallon! I ain't gon' let that nigga just get away with this shit. Even if it means gettin' his daughter involved…" Shantreis shrugged. "Fuck it."

"She's an innocent kid, Treis."

Shantreis narrowed her eyes at her friend. "And my baby wasn't?" She laid back in the bed. "I'm tired now… I'll talk to you tomorrow."

Fallon stared blankly at her cell phone the next day. She had zero missed calls, no new messages… Yesterday she'd sent both Strap and Cash the same message hoping that one—or even both of them would respond, but to her dismay they both ignored her.

I can't believe it… she thought sadly. *A message cursing me out or something would be better than nothing.*

Fallon had been lying in bed all day sulking. Her curtains were drawn so she was completely surrounded in darkness. Her atmosphere mirrored her mood: Gloomy.

It's hard to believe there was once a time in my life when I didn't talk to Cash or Strap… In fact, the more she thought about it, she realized she'd returned to Raleigh five months before she'd reunited with the Hardy brothers.

What the hell did I do back then? Fallon never really hung with her co-workers, preferring to keep her work and personal separate. Besides Shantreis, she didn't have any other friends she really hung out with.

Is this really it? No more Cash… Tears welled up in her eyes. "He really was a good man and my dumb ass messed it up." Fallon stared at her ring and twisted it around her finger. "I ended up hurting two good men… Strap's always been there for me. But what the hell can I do? I love them both."

But I love Cash more, she thought, unable to voice it aloud. *Or do I just feel like I owe him?* It was no secret that Cash had done everything for her throughout the years—he'd been her family when she didn't have one, a security blanket, and so much more. There was no way she could possibly pay him back for everything. *No... Don't be silly. We've been together for three years, of course it's love...*

But, another nagging voice in her head piped up, *They say if you truly love a person then you wouldn't fall for someone else...* Strap had always been a great friend to her, but she knew there was much more than that behind the surface. *If it wasn't then we would've never went as far as we did...*

Reflecting on her conversation with Strap the other day made her wonder. *What would my life have been like if I would've kept his Strap's baby?* Fallon didn't completely believe that her life would've turned out fucked up, but she was afraid... Afraid she'd gotten rid of a life for her own selfish reasons. She shook her head. *No. Don't even think about it. At the end of the day it won't change anything.*

"Ugh," Fallon groaned, clutching her stomach. "What's wrong with—" Feeling the overwhelming need to throw up, she quickly dashed to the toilet. She hadn't been feeling well all morning but she'd attributed it to her mental state.

"Goodness," she cried, wiping her mouth off with a washcloth. *I didn't even eat anything today...* Making her way over to the sink, she quickly gargled to get rid of the lingering acidic taste. *I know I'm not pregnant... Right?*

Quickly she tried to think back to the last time she had her period, but the date was fuzzy. *It can't be... Not now.* The more she thought about it, the more she realized it wasn't entirely impossible. Each time she and Cash had sex, they never bothered to use protection. Fallon wasn't on birth control either. *Cash pulled out though, right?*

Fallon didn't know whether to jump for joy or to cry. *I need to be sure,* she thought. After getting dressed, she rushed out to Target to buy a pregnancy test.

"Where the hell are they at?" she mumbled to herself as she walked down the countless alphanumerical rows. *I give up.* Spotting a woman in a red shirt, Fallon tapped her on the shoulder. "Excuse me, but where are your pregnancy tests?"

"Oh I'm sorry, I don't work—" the woman started before breaking out into a smile. "Fallon, is that you?"

"Taeja." Fallon forced a smile, remembering her from college. While they were definitely more than acquaintances, it would be pushing it to call them friends. She didn't mind talking to her former classmate, but she had more pressing matters to tend to.

"I didn't know you moved back to Raleigh after school!" Taeja glanced down at her hand. "And you're married, too! Wow. Congratulations, girl!"

"Thanks." Fallon didn't bother to correct her. For what? She didn't need to tell everyone her business.

"Look, I'm sure you're busy so I'll keep this short. I'm *really* in need of a job. Do you think you could help me out?" Taeja asked. She could tell just from looking at Fallon that she was doing well. She couldn't say she was surprised. Fallon had always excelled at all her classes in school.

"Yeah sure. Give me your number. I'll let you know because I'm *really* in a rush right now."

"Okay." Taeja reached into her purse and pulled out a piece of paper, scribbling her number on it quickly. "Thank you, Fallon. I really appreciate you looking out for me."

"No problem. I'll let you know something when I go back to work next week." Fallon waved her off quickly then resumed her search. It took her nearly five more minutes before she located the tests. She couldn't get home fast enough.

"C'mon, c'mon," Fallon muttered. She paced back and forth around her bathroom. The two minutes after she'd peed on the stick seemed to be dragging on endlessly. One line had already appeared, but two were required for a positive result.

What will I do if it's positive? Fallon wondered. *I know a baby won't make Cash be with me… or would it?*

The sound of the timer going off snapped her out of her devious thoughts. *Here it goes.* Inhaling deeply, Fallon checked the results.

I can't believe it… What should I do now?

Chapter 5

"Outlaw, I'm tryna tell you I don't have no fuckin' money! These muthafuckas threatenin' to cut off my electricity! You know I don't have anybody else that can help me out!" Kaleesha shouted. She'd been on the phone with him for nearly fifteen minutes but the conversation didn't seem to be going anywhere. He was stubborn as hell.

"Kaleesha, I already told you I don't give a fuck about that shit. Just come pick Monet up. I got some shit to do! You slowin' me down! Damn!" Outlaw cursed. "You ain't seen ya daughter in two fuckin' weeks and all you talkin' about is money!"

"I need money to take care of our daughter. I ain't got much gas in the car either, so you need to make sure you give me—"

"I ain't givin' you shit. Get off ya ass and fuckin' work if you don't wanna be fuckin' poor," he replied coolly. "Matter fact, where's the money you and that pussy ass nigga stole from me? Pay ya bills with that, bitch."

"Fuck you, Outlaw! You know that nigga ain't gimme shit."

"That ain't my fuckin' problem. It don't pay to be a scandalous ass bitch, huh?!" He gazed down at his Hublot watch. "Hurry up and bring ya ass to get Monet. Let me warn you now, don't try to do no dumb shit with her or you'll regret it." Without giving her a chance to respond, he disconnected the line.

"Daddy, I'm hungry," Monet whined, dramatically holding her stomach and lying down on her father's lap.

"What you wanna eat?"

"Mmmm..." She placed a hand under her chin thoughtfully and rubbed it, pretending to mull it over.

Outlaw couldn't help but to laugh at how cute she looked. Monet was always so extra, but that was his baby girl.

"I know! Rainbow confetti pancakes!"

"Daddy doesn't know how to make those."

"Shan-shan does," she said a matter of factly. "Can she come over and make me some?"

"Monet, I told you yesterday. She's not coming back," he stressed. His daughter had been constantly asking about Shantreis despite the many times he'd warned her not to. For whatever reason, it just wasn't getting through to her little brain.

"Why?"

"Cuz she was bad."

"What did she do bad?"

Outlaw sighed, massaging his temple with his free hand. Anytime he thought about Shantreis he got pissed off all over again. "It's grown up stuff."

"Is that why you gave her a whupping?" Monet asked inquisitively.

"I didn't give her a whupping."

"Yes you did. I saw you—"

"Your momma's comin' to get you," he interrupted.

"Really? I really missed Mommy! I wonder if..."

Monet was still talking but Outlaw tuned her out. Once again, Shantreis had unwillingly come to the front of his thoughts. *I wonder if she lost the baby...* He nodded his head. *Probably. I kicked that bitch hard as hell.* For a millisecond, a twinge of remorse washed over him, but it left as quickly as it came. *Fuck it. Bitch deserved that shit. And if the fuckin' police show up to my doorstep, she's gonna wish I had killed her too.*

"**B**ae, I'm starvin'!" Malaysia whined. She and Ghost were driving down Falls of Neuse on the way home, but she wanted to make a detour.

"Then get somethin' to eat," Ghost snorted. "What the fuck you tellin' me for?"

"I wanna go somewhere nice. Can't we go to *The Cheesecake Factory?*" she asked, stopping at a light. "You promised me we would but we ain't gone yet."

"Man, fuck that. Cook Out right there."

Malaysia rolled her eyes. "I'm tired of eatin' at the damn Cook Out."

"Then just—" Ghost lost his train of thought when he saw a canary yellow Camaro pull into the parking lot of the restaurant. "Ay, pull in and drop me off by the door." He pulled his gray hoodie low over his head. "Wait for me at the exit, a'ight?"

"Ghost, what the fuck you about to do?"

"Send a message to these niggas. Now hurry the fuck up." Ghost recognized the Camaro as belonging to Quon, one of his brother's workers. *Or should I say one of Outlaw's workers,* he thought. Ghost still felt some type of way about all the money he was missing out on.

After Malaysia let him out, Ghost wasted no time making his way towards Quon's car. He was second in line. Ghost wanted to catch him before he placed his order. It was daytime but the sky outside was cloudy. The weather forecasts were reporting rain, but Ghost didn't give a fuck. Even if the sun was shining, he'd still handle his business. Although there was a higher risk of getting caught, it gave him an adrenaline rush. He was in his notorious I-don't-give-a-fuck-about-shit mode.

Walking briskly with his hand on his concealed .45, Ghost swiftly opened the passenger door to Quon's car just as he was about to pull up.

"Man, what the fuck!" Quon exclaimed. "Are you—?"

Ghost smirked devilishly as he pushed his gun roughly against Quon's skull. "Damn, homie, caught you slippin'." He laughed obnoxiously, reveling in the apparent fear on his victim's face. "Now don't fuckin' move or I'll murk your ass. You already know how I get down, my nigga. I ain't got no type of regard for human life, right?" he said, quoting what his brother had told him once.

"Yeah. Just chill, man. I got my son with me."

Ghost didn't bother to look. He'd already peeped the boy in the backseat when he'd made his way towards the car. "Then I guess you better do everything I fuckin' say so he won't have to watch his daddy die, right?"

"What you want, Ghost? Money?" He searched his eyes for confirmation but didn't find any.

"Nah. Do I look like a broke nigga to you, muh'fucka?"

"Then what is it?" Quon shook slightly. *How am I gonna get myself out of this shit?*

Quon wanted to look back and check on his son, but didn't want to inadvertently provoke Ghost. He was unpredictable. There was no way Quon could trust that he wouldn't kill him. Ghost was bold enough to stick a gun to his head at a drive thru, after all. His eyes moved slightly towards the sideview mirror, hoping someone would come behind him and see what was going on.

"I just want you to tell my brother something," Ghost said. "That's all."

Quon looked at him apprehensively. "Yeah?"

"Just tell him I'm back in town. Not too hard is it?"

"N-nah."

"Good." Ghost gave his infamous mischievous smile before hitting Quon with the butt of his gun, swiftly rendering him unconscious. Just as Quon's foot slipped off the brake, Ghost let himself out and jogged towards Malaysia's waiting Benz.

Malaysia had been fucking with Ghost long enough to know not to ask any questions, so when he entered the car, she was silent. Her eyes did the talking when she peered into the rearview mirror just in time to see a yellow Camaro crash into one of the parked cars in the lot. She pulled out just as she heard the screams. Ghost turned up the radio to drown it out.

"Nah, nah nah... Tell me what happened again," Blaze sneered as he looked over at Shantreis. He'd just picked her up from the hospital but she'd refused to tell him anything until she got inside the car. "I must've heard some shit wrong… This pussy ass nigga *kicked* you in the fuckin' stomach then *dragged* you to the fuckin' curb like you was trash or some shit?"

It was his fifty millionth time asking Shantreis that question, but each time she obliged him. It was her goal to ensure he got as riled up as possible so her plan could go through without a hitch. It also helped that she exaggerated certain aspects of the story.

Since I know I can't depend on Fallon's scary ass, she thought. Shantreis nodded her head. "Yup. That's exactly how it happened. One of the neighbors found me on the side of the road and called the ambulance. The doctor said if they hadn't been so quick, I could've died from blood loss."

"Wow…" Vexed, Blaze beat his fists against the steering wheel. He'd planned on taking her back to his house but after all that she'd told him, Blaze was going to take a little detour. "I thought some crazy shit might a' happened to you yesterday when you ain't pick up ya fuckin' phone! Damn, Treis! I could a' handled this shit yesterday!"

Nah, I need to be there, Shantreis thought. "I just wasn't in the mood," she lied. "I was tired and mad at the whole fuckin' world."

Blaze looked over at Shantreis again, studying the bruises on her face. "He fucked you up…"

"Yeah." Shantreis sighed sullenly. She pulled down the sun visor to look in the mirror. Her face was still fucked up, but she wasn't expecting it to look much better after only one day. Her bottom lip was still swollen and there were bruises on her face from where he'd hit her. She'd tried covering them up with makeup but for the most part they were still visible.

"You sure the doctor said the baby's gonna be straight?"

She nodded. "Yeah. He just said I gotta take it easy and I should be able to carry it to term without any problems." Shantreis placed a hand on her small belly. She couldn't believe it when the doctor told her that she was fifteen weeks because she sure didn't look it. *My damn nose is getting wider though,* she thought with a frown.

Noticing they weren't going in the direction of Blaze's house, Shantreis turned to him nervously. "Did you move or something? Where are we goin'?"

"Where you think? To that pussy nigga house!"

"What the fuck you gonna do?!" Shantreis demanded. "Do you even have a plan?! Outlaw crazy as hell!"

"So am I! He fucked with the wrong one! I still owe him for last time, too!" Blaze hadn't forgotten about their first encounter when Outlaw pulled a gun out on him. "You remember that shit?"

"Yeah I remember."

"Never let a nigga live after you pull a gun on him," he murmured, "You would think that nigga would know that... Now he's gonna regret that shit."

"So..." The closer they got to Outlaw's house, the more Shantreis's nerves started fucking with her. "What are you gonna do? You gonna kill him then?"

Blaze looked at her mischievously. "You want me to? You think it's worth his life?" The tone in his voice suggested he was asking for permission, but Shantreis couldn't get a good read on him.

Is this nigga joking? Shantreis wondered. She had known Blaze for most of his life. He was far from a killer. *He was always robbing niggas and shit, but he ain't never killed nobody.* She gave him the side eye. *At least not to my knowledge.*

"Blaze, you ain't never killed a nigga in your life! It ain't as easy to pull the trigger as you think."

"Speaking from experience?" he asked curiously.

"No," she answered quickly. "I'm just sayin'... You got a gun?"

"I'm a convicted felon, Treis. What do you think?"

Shantreis raised an eyebrow. "So is that a no?" When he didn't answer, she immediately panicked. "Oh hell no!" She shook her head. "Turn the fuckin' car around, Blaze! You gonna fuck around and get both of us killed!"

"You think that nigga stupid enough to shoot me out in the fuckin' open?" he snapped. "Chill the fuck out."

Man, hell nah. This nigga gotta be smokin' somethin' if he don't realize how stupid this shit sounds, Shantreis thought. "Fuck that shit you talkin'. I got my own plan to get back at him."

"What?"

"His daughter."

Now it was Blaze's turn to raise his eyebrow and look at Shantreis like she was crazy. "What the fuck type shit are you on?"

"We'd just kidnap her and—"

"Nah, Treis. No good. I don't fuck with people's kids. That's some coward ass shit." He shook his head as he continued to chastise her, "That's a bad fuckin' idea."

"Yours ain't much better! You don't know the type of nigga Outlaw is evidently. He got his nickname for a reason."

"Do I look like I give a fuck? There ain't a nigga on this earth that can put fear in my fuckin' heart," Blaze assured her as he boldly parked on the side of Outlaw's lawn. "C'mon." He shut the car off and opened his door.

"Nah. I'm good. You're on your own," Shantreis told him just as raindrops splattered across the windshield. "And leave the keys."

"You scary as hell," he chuckled.

"Whatever."

Shantreis watched in anticipation as he stalked up to the front door. Blaze pounded his fists against the door loudly like he was the police.

"Open up, fuck nigga!" Blaze roared. Lightning cracked loudly in the distance, lighting up the sky just as Shantreis saw the door open. Her mouth widened to see a gun appear first, followed by Outlaw's scowling face.

I tried to tell him, she thought. Shantreis wanted to get out of the car, but her feet felt cemented to the floor.

"Nigga, ya girl ain't tell you that I would kill yo' ass if you showed up on my porch?" Outlaw asked with a smirk, pointing his 9 millimeter directly at his dome.

Blaze shrugged. "You can't tell I don't give a fuck?" He nodded towards Outlaw's gun before raising his own fists. "Let me find out you scared to throw them hands. Shit… Last time at the club you was hidin' behind ya pistol, too. You was quick to put ya hands on my baby momma though!"

Outlaw's jaw flexed in irritation. "Fuck—"

"Daddy!" Monet called, making her way to the front door. "It's thunderin' and I'm scared!"

"Go to your room right fuckin' now!" Outlaw shouted, feeling her small arms wrap around his leg in fear.

"Daddy, I'm scared!" she sobbed. His harsh tone combined with seeing the gun in his hand frightened her.

"It's okay. I was just leaving, sweetheart," Blaze explained, noticing how Outlaw's guard had gone down at the arrival of his daughter.

Outlaw placed his gun in the back of his jeans and scooped his daughter up. "This is yo' final warning, nigga. If you bring ya ass back over here then you gon' be leavin' in a trash bag."

Blaze nodded his head mockingly, but leaving was the last thing on his mind. *Not until I settle the score,* he thought.

As soon as Outlaw started closing the door, Blaze forcefully pushed the door back on him. The door struck him in the face, momentarily dazing him and causing Monet to drop from his arms. Moving quickly, Blaze grabbed him and punched him fiercely. Blood spewed from his mouth and flew onto the light-colored wall.

"Ooh shit," Shantreis gasped from the car. Blaze disappeared inside, leaving the front door wide open but she couldn't see from where she sat. "Fuck this." She hurried out of the car and into the house. *I don't wanna miss this shit!*

"Shan-shan!" Monet squealed the moment she saw her. "That man!!"

Shantreis closed the door behind her and stepped into the foyer. She turned to her right to see the two men tussling and tearing up the living room. Despite Blaze's smaller stature, he was capable of holding his own. He'd gotten more than a few good licks in. That was until Outlaw threw a strong haymaker at Blaze. It struck him so hard Shantreis could've sworn she heard his jaw break.

"Fuck nigga!" Outlaw spat—literally. The blood tinged spit hit Blaze directly in the face. Although Blaze had gotten a head start, he'd lost his advantage.

"Pussy ass nigga! You think you just gon' come in my house and beat my fuckin' ass?! Nigga, you crazy!" Outlaw shouted, pinning Blaze underneath him. Using a gun might have been his main preference, but he'd been in many fist fights growing up.

As Blaze tried to get up, Outlaw pressed his forearm against his windpipe forcefully. "Now I'm gonna murk ya ass just for trespassing on my fuckin' property!"

Fuck, Shantreis thought. *What the fuck can I do? Think, Treis, think!* Monet's screaming combined with their fighting was messing with her concentration. *I gotta find a weapon!* Swiftly she dashed out the room.

"Stop it, Daddy!" Monet screamed, but Outlaw didn't appear to hear her. He was in his own world.

"Any last words, muthafucka?" Outlaw grinned before reaching into the back of his jeans for his gun. *I think I'm a' give this nigga a closed casket funeral.* He aimed straight for Blaze's head.

BLAOW!!!

Chapter 6

"Uhm…" Fallon looked back at her phone screen in disbelief. She could've sworn she called Cash's phone, but there had to be some sort of mistake if a female was picking up. "I'm sorry. I must have the wrong number…" *Did he change his number just so he wouldn't have to talk to me?*

"Who were you trying to reach?" the woman asked innocently.

"Cash… But I must've dialed—"

"No. You got the right one. This is his phone." On the other end of the line, Remy grinned. She didn't even bother to contain her laughter. Cash was still over her house after she'd persuaded him to stay the night. "But he's currently in the shower. Would you like to leave a message?"

"Who is this?" Fallon demanded, immediately reverting to jealous girlfriend mode. *We just broke up yesterday and already he's seeing another female?!*

"Remy."

"Remy?" she repeated in shock. "He's with *you*?"

He still keeps in touch with her? Maybe there was more to the story than I thought since he's still messing with her now...

Fallon remembered the girl all too well. It was because of Remy she ended up sleeping with Strap that year ago. It was her own secret payback for when she'd first heard what he'd done. It was a memory she tried to repress, especially since she'd never spoken a word of it to Cash before. He still had no clue that she knew.

"You say it like it's a problem. They say the way you get him is the way you'll lose him," Remy added casually.

"You say it like he was your man," Fallon snapped back. "Just put him on the phone! It's important!"

"He was! Me and Cash got history, or were you unaware?" Remy countered, ignoring Fallon's request. "If you think our first time fuckin' was last year then you really don't know shit." Fallon was silent. Remy smiled, knowing she'd successfully gotten under her skin. "Lemme tell you some more shit you ain't know—"

Before Remy could finish her statement, Cash snatched the phone from her grasp and immediately disconnected the line.

"Now see, that's the reason why I quit fuckin' with you in the first place... You love that drama shit." He sighed as he took a seat on the edge of the bed.

"No, Cash, you *brought* that drama shit to *my* doorstep." Remy pointed a perfectly manicured nail at him. "You might wanna call ol' girl back though. She said it's important," she added sarcastically.

"I'll call her back later." No sooner than the words left his mouth, his phone started vibrating again. To no surprise, Fallon was calling him back. Cash flashed Remy an annoyed look before standing up and walking out of the room. "Don't follow me either."

"This is exactly what the fuck I be talkin' about! Don't talk to that bitch when you in my house! That's disrespectful as fuck and you know it."

"Disrespectful?" he asked incredulously. "Nah. Disrespectful is answerin' a nigga phone when nobody gave yo' ass permission."

Remy pouted silently. She crossed her arms, knowing he had a point. Normally she would've continued to argue with him but today she would let it go.

"What, Fallon?" Cash asked when he answered the phone.

"You moved on already? With *her?*" Fallon quizzed. Hurt was present in her voice. She had to bite down on her lip to stop a sob from escaping.

"Fallon, who I choose to spend my time with is none of your concern. Our shit is dead. I don't even know why you callin' my phone. What the hell is so important?"

"Just call me back when you're alone…"

"I'm done with you, Fallon, so why the fuck would I call you back? If you need somethin' then call my brother." His tone was harsh and indifferent.

"You're such an asshole, Cash."

"Is that it?"

"Yeah. That's it! You can just pretend me and the baby don't exist!" *Click.*

"What?" Cash yelled after her, but she'd already disconnected the line. *Did she say 'the baby'?* Quickly he called her back, but now she wasn't answering.

"Everything okay?" Remy asked curiously. She'd tried her best to ear hustle but couldn't make out anything Fallon said.

"Ay, I'm a' holla at you later," Cash told Remy. He brushed past her to the bedroom. There were a million questions running through his mind and only Fallon had the answers.

"Wait! Where are you goin'?" she panicked, noticing Cash was putting his clothes back on. He had promised to take her out for brunch but it was clear their date was cancelled. *I guess he's gonna go see that bitch,* she thought bitterly.

Cash didn't respond as he slipped his shoes on. He continued to dial Fallon's number even as he exited the house. After being sent repeatedly to voicemail, he figured she'd powered her phone off.

Oh well. I'll have to pay her a visit then… Either way, we're gonna talk about this shit. A baby? Damn. I thought I was done with Fallon! Now I have to deal with her for eighteen fuckin' years? If it's even mine… Cruel thoughts invaded his mind. *For all I know that's Strap's baby. I caught them yesterday but that don't mean they ain't been fuckin' with each other…*

"**D**addy! Get up! Get up!" Monet shrieked. Seeing her father lying down with blood pooling around him was the most frightening sight ever for a three-year-old child.

Outlaw tried to speak but only managed to gurgle up his own blood.

Shantreis looked over at him. Outlaw appeared to still be breathing, but she knew that wouldn't last long. After all, she'd shot him in the chest. When she saw Blaze was losing, she had to do something. Outlaw kept guns stashed all around the house, always prepared for anything. In no time she'd retrieved the .9mm he kept in the drawer of an end table in the family room.

I didn't want to kill him, but it's too late for that. She'd aimed for his shoulder but ended up hitting his chest instead. *If it wasn't him, then it would've been us.* Shantreis truly believed it yet her emotions were mixed about what she'd done.

"Damn, Treis," Blaze muttered, sitting up a couple of feet away from where Outlaw lay. He was still struggling to remain conscious. "I spent five years of my life locked up and—"

Shantreis narrowed her eyes at him. "Nigga, what?! You are aware he was about to kill your ass, right?" *Ungrateful bastard.* "I guess I should've just let him, right? I *know* Outlaw! If I hadn't killed him then he would've killed us! If we lived then we would've been living on the run from him! I don't know about you but I'm not wasting my life like that."

"Shut the fuck up, Treis. That ain't what I'm sayin'!" Blaze shook his head. "You don't think the neighbors heard the shit? You don't think somebody's gonna call the police?"

"They probably thought it was thunder." She shrugged her shoulders disinterestedly. "Even if they think it's a gun, they don't know where the hell it came from."

"What about her?" Blaze nodded his head in Monet's direction. The girl was still crying over her father, willing him to get up. "I can't believe you shot him in front of his fuckin' daughter. That shit was foul!"

Shantreis rolled her eyes. "Damn, nigga. You still ain't thanked me for savin' your fuckin' life. Goin' to jail made you soft and scary as hell."

"Shut the fuck up, Shantreis. You just ain't got no fuckin' common sense! You think she ain't gonna say nothin'? Be for real! Or you gon' murk a kid too?" he added mockingly.

Before Shantreis could answer, Monet came running in her direction.

"Shan-Shan!!!!" she screamed hysterically. She tugged at Shantreis's arm. Snot was running down her nose and her little eyes were puffy from all the crying she'd been doing. "My Daddy's hurt! My Mommy said you call 911 when somebody's hurt!!!" Monet ran for the phone but Shantreis grabbed her.

"Stop, Monet! We can't do that." Shantreis stooped down, becoming eye level with the child. "Be quiet! Listen to me!" She shook her slightly. "Your daddy was a bad man. Bad things happen to bad people, sweetie."

"My daddy wasn't a—"

"Yes he was!" she shouted sharply. "Now remember this, if you don't want bad things to happen to you too, you'll keep your mouth shut!"

Instantly Monet was quiet, sniffling softly. She was truly terrified by Shantreis's words.

"Any more questions?" Shantreis asked Blaze sarcastically.

Blaze shook his head, but his look was still disapproving.

"Go to the Maserati and put Outlaw in the trunk. We'll ditch his body in Franklinton. I know this abandoned house off Main Street where we can put him."

When we come back then I'll get the money, she thought. Outlaw didn't keep much stashed at their house but it would be enough for now. *Then I'll sell the townhouse and get my own place. Start over fresh.* Shantreis smiled. *I'd say this was better payback than takin' Monet.*

"Ay, get me a garbage bag," Blaze directed. "Y'all got the big black ones?"

"Yeah."

"Get me some. I'm a' put it under this nigga and line the trunk so he won't fuck it up."

Shantreis quickly did as she was told. *Maybe Blaze has done somethin' like this before.* Despite his initial reprimanding, he was calm and composed.

"I'll drive the Maserati so that way if anybody sees us, nobody will suspect anything." She nodded towards Monet. "I'll take her with me. You just follow behind us, okay?"

Blaze nodded his head. He headed for the front door while Shantreis took Monet by the hand and led her to the garage.

"Are we taking Daddy to the hospital?" Monet eked out, looking at Shantreis cautiously.

"Didn't I say keep your mouth shut?!" she snapped. "Don't say *anything* else about your dad!"

Monet whimpered in response as she got into her car seat and waited for Shantreis to buckle her in.

Shantreis hated how cruel she was treating the little girl, but what choice did she have? *Blaze was right. We can't let her say shit or who knows what the fuck will happen? Getting caught by the police or getting caught by Cash... I don't know which one is worse. Either way, I can't let that shit happen.*

She hit the garage door opener and started to back out, but a blacked out Navigator blocked her exit.

Who the fuck is that?

Shantreis didn't have to wonder for long. Holding an umbrella over her head, Kaleesha stepped out from the passenger side. Briskly she approached the Maserati with a frown on her face. Shantreis pulled down her window in annoyance.

"Where is Outlaw?" Kaleesha peered nosily into the car, disappointed when there was no sign of her child's father.

"He's inside… Sleep," Shantreis added quickly.

"Well, he better wake his ass up!" Kaleesha went to the door, pounding on it. "Outlaw!!! Where's my muthafuckin' money?"

Shantreis sighed and got out of the car. "What the hell are you doin' here?! You must didn't understand when Outlaw told your ass not to—"

"No!" Kaleesha whirled around to face her. "Outlaw told me to come over and get Monet. *That's* why I'm here. He promised he would give me some money too!"

She looked at her quizzically, wondering if she was telling the truth. *He wouldn't have, would he? Fuck it. I'll just go with the flow.* "Oh… He must've decided that when I was gone. You can get Monet out the back but Outlaw said he ain't givin' you no money."

"He better!" Kaleesha tried to beat on the door again but Shantreis jerked her away.

"Get your daughter and go!"

"Bitch! Don't put your fuckin' hands on me!"

"Then get the fuck out of my garage!"

"Not until I see Outlaw!"

"Kaleesha! Hurry the fuck up, girl!" a voice boomed from the Navigator. "I ain't got all fuckin' day!"

Shantreis did a double take. "You bringin' niggas over here, too? Yeah. You really need to hurry up and go! You know Outlaw don't play that shit!" She'd said it so convincingly that even she believed it. It was true, but of course there was nothing Outlaw could or would do about it.

Kaleesha rolled her eyes. "That's my brother Tony." She turned back to him. "I'm coming!"

Tony didn't fuck with her much, preferring to stay out of her business. Today was a rare exception. Since her car was currently in the shop and her girlfriends were unavailable, he'd offered to take her to Outlaw's house. The one condition was that she hurried since he had to go to work in an hour.

"I know you got some money—" Kaleesha started.

"Not for you I don't." Shantreis nodded her head towards Monet. "Get your daughter and go. You haven't seen her in forever and all you're worried about is a nigga."

"Whatever." Kaleesha opened the back door and greeted her daughter with a hug. "Mo-Mo! Mommy really missed you, sweetie!" She held Monet tightly, but noticed her sad face. "What's wrong, baby? Did you miss me too?"

Monet nodded but the depressed expression on her face remained. As Kaleesha carried her towards their car, Shantreis called after them.

"Bye, Monet. You be a good girl, okay?" Shantreis hoped Monet picked up on the underlying warning in her tone. "If you're bad then you know what will happen..."

Monet nodded her head solemnly. Shantreis smiled. *Maybe we won't have to worry about her...*

Chapter 7

"Strap... What are you doin' here?" Fallon asked, surprised to see him at her door.

"Look, man, honestly... Yesterday I wanted to say 'fuck you'," Strap admitted sincerely. "And I know you said you needed your space but look, I had to see you... I had to talk to you. Can I come in?"

"Oh yeah," she said nervously, stepping aside. Fallon had gotten a text message from Cash a couple of minutes ago stating he was on the way. *This is gonna be a big mess if both of them are here at the same time...* She hadn't easily forgotten how their run in yesterday morning could've turned out. But what could she do? Fallon didn't want to tell him to leave. The vulnerable look on his handsome face melted her heart.

Strap embraced Fallon tightly, inhaling her familiar scent deeply. "About yesterday..." he started.

"I'm sorry," she interjected, feeling guilty for her earlier actions. "I really didn't want to hurt you. I didn't mean all of those mean things I said to you either. I just hated how you were making me feel! Back when everything went down, it seemed like everyone was judging me. It really hurt when you did too because I didn't expect that from you! Not my Damien… the one who worshipped the ground I walked on."

Fallon took a deep breath, willing herself not to cry as she made her next confession. "Did you know I couldn't stop crying the day I got the abortion? I kept convincing myself I did the right thing… That I *had* to do it for school… I *had* to if I wanted my life to stay the same… Even though I tried to rationalize it, I couldn't stop thinking about it. I wondered what our child would've looked like and…" She stifled the sob threatening to escape her throat. "I felt like shit! Yesterday, you made me relive that all over again! It hurt so I wanted make you feel as bad as I did."

Strap clung to her tighter, rocking her back and forth gently. "I'm sorry, baby. That shit really fucked with a nigga though." He kissed her on the forehead. "Fuck the past. I thought about it for a while and decided it really doesn't matter what happened two years ago." He smiled. "It's gonna sound corny as hell, but the only thing that matters is the future… I really wanna build one with you. I know you need some time to yourself and I can respect that."

Tears stung Fallon's eyelids as Strap bared his soul to her. His sincerity touched her deeply. "Really?"

"Yeah. I…" His voice trailed off as his eyes focused on her coffee table. "Damn… Is that a pregnancy test?"

Shit, Fallon thought. She'd had it out in preparation for Cash's arrival. *I should've put it up before I answered the door!* Nodding her head, she pulled away from his embrace.

"Is it—?"

"Yeah. It's Cash's," she choked out nervously.

Strap made his way over to her living room, staring intently at the stick. "Damn… When did you find out?"

"I just found out this morning."

"Wow…" He flopped down on her sofa, deep in thought. *Damn.*

"You don't want me anymore do you?" Fallon asked, her eyes glazed over tears.

After a long uncomfortable silence, Strap finally spoke, "Are you gonna keep it?"

"I don't know… Do you *want* me to get rid of it?"

"I could never ask you to do that, Fallon. I would *never* do that. That's my blood in there." Strap looked at her. "Does Cash already know?"

"Well, sort of. I called him but we didn't really talk about it. I'm trying to figure out what I want to do."

"You should keep it," he said quickly. "My brother is a lot of things, but I know he'll take responsibility. I'm sure of that. Either way… I got you, okay?"

Fallon nodded. "Thank you, Damien. But what about you and me? You never answered my question."

"What? Do I still want you?" he asked incredulously. Realizing that was exactly what she was curious about, he alleviated her fears. "Yeah, Fallon. Of course. I want every part of you."

Fallon smiled, knowing he was referring to the baby as well. Her heart swelled with love and admiration. *Damien never ceases to amaze me. He has such a big heart.* She knew she didn't have it in her to be that accepting. If he'd told her he had a baby on the way, Fallon probably would have childishly asked him to choose. *He's definitely more mature than most men at his age.*

"When I said I love you, Fallon, I meant that shit." Strap stood up and hugged her again. "Don't ever doubt me again, a'ight?"

Fallon returned the embrace, but once again she felt conflicted. *Just earlier today I thought I would choose Cash, but then Strap keeps stepping up and showing me why he's a better man… Cash is back with that bitch Remy so I guess I should just forget about him anyway.*

An old saying sprung to her mind: If you can't be with the one you love, love the one you're with.

She nodded. *Yeah… That's what I'll do.*

"I might—" Fallon started, but the knock on the door interrupted her. *Uh oh…*

Strap looked at her curiously. "You expectin' company?" Before she could respond, he started for the door. Fallon stood nervously, wringing her hands anxiously.

"You told Cash to come over?" he asked. Strap placed his hand on the doorknob and peered through the peephole.

"I didn't tell him to," she replied in a small voice. "He texted me saying he was coming over… He wanted to talk about the baby I guess."

"You want me to stay or go?"

"Uh… Maybe it's a conversation we should have privately."

"A'ight." Strap nodded his head in understanding as he opened the door.

"Damn," Cash cursed under his breath. *Fallon had the nerve to question me about Remy but I see she's still fuckin' with my brother.* He couldn't say he'd expected her not to, but seeing Strap at the door reignited the fire he'd started yesterday.

Fallon came to Strap's side and opened the door wider, allowing Cash access inside. "I'll talk to you later, Strap."

"Yeah." The brothers exchanged one last set of tense glances before Strap exited.

"So what's up?" Cash asked. An irritated expression was on his face. "What's that shit you was talkin' about on the phone? You pregnant?" He took a seat at her bar. There was no way he could bring himself to sit on the same sofa they'd presumably fucked on.

"Yes," she squeaked. "I found out earlier today." Fallon handed him the test, watching him nervously while he silently examined it.

After what seemed like an eternity, Cash finally spoke, "You sure it's mine?"

Fallon scowled. "Yes I'm sure!" She was offended. How could he think otherwise? "I only slept with you, Cash!"

He snickered cynically. "You gettin' mad and shit, but how the fuck do I know that for sure? Honestly if I hadn't walked in on y'all yesterday, nobody would've told me shit!" Cash silently dared her to lie to him. She looked like she wanted to protest, but he continued, "Now whether or not you would a' broke up with me is another discussion, but I know damn well you *wouldn't* have said shit. I don't know how many times y'all done fucked before I found out about it."

"It was just once," she lied. Fallon meant it when she said she'd never tell Cash about her and Strap's rendezvous years ago. "It was a mistake."

"A mistake?" Cash repeated in disbelief. He shook his head. "Get the fuck outta here. You don't fuck another nigga by mistake, Fallon."

"Your opinion about that is irrelevant, Damontrez. All that matters is the current situation. What do you want me to do? Do you want me to get rid of it?"

Cash shrugged his shoulders. "I don't care what you do."

Whoa, Fallon thought. The conversation wasn't going anywhere in the direction she'd thought. *I should have told Strap to stay.* He'd seemed so sure Cash would be willing to take responsibility but it was just the opposite. She barely recognized the man sitting in front of her. *I can't believe he would say that. I know he's mad but damn...*

"Why the fuck did you come over here if you didn't care?!" she yelled.

"If you decide to keep it and it's mine, I'll take care of it," he answered coolly, unfazed by her shouting. He narrowed his eyebrows. "I don't want that nigga around though."

"If we're together, then Strap *will* be around our child," Fallon scoffed. "I bet you'll have that bitch Remy around our child! You're being real childish right now, Damontrez."

"I don't care," Cash responded indifferently. "That nigga is his fuckin' uncle and you're probably gonna have him playin' Daddy to my seed!"

Fallon shook her head, stunned by Cash's cold behavior. "What I did was fucked up, but do you have to act like this? It's not about me, it's about our child!" she shouted, matching his tone. Fallon was past fed up with his attitude. *Maybe he's right... I don't know but I'm not gonna let him keep talking to me like this.*

Cash stood up and stalked over to her, standing directly in front of her. "What do you want me to say, Fallon? You fucked everything up! I ain't never wanna be on no baby daddy, baby momma shit with you! You was supposed to be my fuckin' wife! Instead you fucked my brother and pregnant with my seed! This sounds like some shit off Jerry Springer!

"What the fuck did you think I was gonna do—say I'm happy or some shit? I can barely stand to look at yo' ass now! Every time I do I think about what you did! The fact you still with that nigga makes it even worse! That's how I *know* it wasn't a fuckin' mistake! You love that nigga, Fallon, whether or not you wanna tell me the shit!

"And you wanna talk about fucked up? Let me tell you what's fucked up! I *loved* you more than any other female I ever been with and you betrayed me! I always looked out for *both* of my brothers and they both tried to take a nigga life! Ghost tried to kill me and Strap took my life with you! If I ain't give a fuck about you I would a' just brushed the shit off but I can't! I really hate yo' ass for that, Fallon!"

Cash felt a small sense of relief after he'd finished. He'd finally gotten it off his chest. He said everything he'd wanted to tell Fallon yesterday.

"I'm sorry, Damontrez!" Tears slid down Fallon's cheeks like a dam that had just burst. Hearing the vulnerability and pain in his voice really affected her. "I am so so sorry. How many times do I have to tell you that?!" She tried to hug him but he backed away as if her touch was poisonous.

"Don't apologize. It don't mean shit!"

"You act like you've never fucked up or made any mistakes during our relationship! You have but I still forgave you!"

"When have I ever fucked up?" Cash looked at her curiously. "Because I was slangin' and you ain't like it?" He waved her off. "That ain't shit."

"You're right. It's not. But this is." Fallon narrowed her eyes, stopping the waterfall of tears so quickly that Cash wondered if she'd been acting. "The way you did Remy…" His puzzled expression only confirmed Fallon's thoughts. "I didn't wanna believe it back then, but now I'm seeing that side of you."

"What are you talkin' about?"

"How you got her pregnant and paid her off to make her abort it," she explained.

"Who told you——?"

"Exactly," Fallon huffed. "So don't act like you haven't fucked up and regretted it too!"

Chapter 8

"Ay!" Ghost called behind Malaysia, "Get me some Cigarillos, too!"

"If you wanna make requests and shit, you should a' brought yo' ass in the store!" Malaysia rolled her eyes at him. They were at the Sheetz gas station on Thornton Road. *He got me out in this dreary ass, wet ass weather,* she thought.

"I'm payin' for the got damn shit!" he yelled back. He perched against the side of the car, smoking a blunt. "I just gave her my last hundred… Fuck." Ghost was in desperate need of a come up. Sure, he could rob more niggas—that's how he'd been making it so far, but that shit was temporary. Most times the money only lasted a day.

Ghost was starting to regret the way he used to blow money. *Hell, the shit used to come so fast that it didn't fuckin' matter.* Immediately his mind went back to Outlaw and Cash. To him, they were the cause of all of his problems. *Fuck them niggas.*

It was then that a blue Maserati pulled up to an empty pump a couple of feet away from him. The license plate read 'Out1@w'. Even without it Ghost would've recognized whose whip it was. *Speak of the fuckin' devil.*

He watched Shantreis exit the car and head inside the gas station. Since the windows were tinted he couldn't see inside, but he would bet money Outlaw wasn't with her. *This shit will be easy as hell. I know that bitch keep a couple stacks on her at a time.* Smiling widely, he made his way to the car. Although he didn't have any beef with Shantreis, he was still going to rob her. *Hell, anybody can get it. Nothing personal.*

The next thing Ghost saw gave him pause. *What the fuck?* The trunk of the car had opened but no one was around. As he stepped closer and peered inside, he saw Outlaw lying down inside. Black trash bags were underneath him. Ghost could see the familiar hole of a bullet in his shirt. *What the fuck type shit is shawty on?*

"H-Help…" Outlaw managed weakly. His vision was blurry. He felt himself losing consciousness, but he mustered up the last of his strength to pull the emergency trunk release button.

I ain't goin' out like no pussy, Outlaw thought.

"Fallon, you must a' heard some shit wrong," Cash argued. "Who told you that shit?"

"Does it matter?" She folded her arms, trying to read his facial expression.

"If she told you that shit then she's a got damn liar—" He began, but his phone going off interrupted him. Reading Quon's name on the screen, he quickly pressed ignore. Whatever he wanted could wait.

Cash took a deep breath. He hadn't wanted to tell Fallon the truth but it didn't matter anymore, right? *Fuck it. I might as well.* "Here's what really happened—" Once again his phone rang.

"Hold up, Fallon." Cash picked up the phone, answering in an exasperated tone. "Yeah, Quon. What's up?"

"We all out," Quon informed, speaking in codes. "Outlaw said he was on his way a couple of hours ago to restock but he still ain't came through. I called the nigga but he ain't pickin' up."

Cash hadn't spoken to Outlaw all day either, but he had been too preoccupied to hit him up. *That ain't like him though...* Something was wrong. Outlaw spent most of his time in the hood even when he didn't have to. His dedication to the game was unmatched. "I'm a' look into it and hit you back."

"Ay, it's one more thing you should know. Ghost back."

"What? Are you sure?"

"Yeah, man! Nigga pulled up on me when I was with my muthafuckin' kid."

Fallon wasn't sure what they were talking about, but knew it had to be bad from the incensed expression on Cash's face.

"A'ight." Cash nodded his head. "I'll handle it." He disconnected the line and turned to Fallon. "I'll holla at you later."

"Wait!" she called after him. "Tell me the truth! What was up with you and Remy?"

Cash sighed. "She was pregnant but she ain't get an abortion…" His eyes were full of guilt. "It was my fault though."

"What do you mean?" Fallon questioned, but Cash was already walking out of the door.

Ghost smirked. "Fuck happened to you, nigga?" Outlaw opened his mouth to speak, but it was a rhetorical question. Immediately Ghost struck him roughly upside the head, rendering him unconscious.

Why she ain't tied this nigga up? How long this nigga been back here? I'm surprised he ain't dead yet! Hell, did she know he was back here? It sounded crazy but he'd seen it happen before. Hell, he'd even done it a few times before. *Either way, some muh'fucka got to the nigga before I could. Oh well. That's how the game goes.*

"Excuse me! Who are you and what are you doin'?!" Shantreis panicked, rushing over. She didn't want to draw too much attention to herself but what else could she do? "Get away from my car!"

Ghost slammed down the trunk. "What's up, Treis?" he probed.

"G-G-Ghost," Shantreis stuttered. She hadn't recognized him until she drew closer. *I thought he left. All this nigga did was cut his hair! Dammit! Why did it have to be him of all people?*

"Damn. It never surprises me just how grimy you bitches are."

Shantreis eyed him warily, trying to be careful of her wording. Ghost was a loose cannon. The last thing she wanted was for him to explode. "What's up, Ghost? How you doin'?"

"Better than Outlaw," he answered. "Now I wonder what the fuck you would a' did if I wasn't here?" His grin grew wider as a car pulled up at the pump next to them.

"Thank you, Ghost," she said through clenched teeth. "I appreciate it." She reached for the gas pump but he beat her to it.

"Nah. I got you," he assured.

Shantreis cut straight to the chase. "What do you want from me?"

"How much was that worth—me savin' yo' ass just now?"

"I got less than a thousand in cash on me, Ghost."

"You straight?" a male's voice suddenly entered the conversation.

Damn it, Blaze, Shantreis thought. *He's gonna make shit worse if he gets involved.* While Ghost's head was turned to face Blaze, she quickly began making frantic motions with her hands. "Everything's fine."

"This you?" Ghost asked.

"Yeah. Somethin' like that," Blaze replied. He sized Ghost up. He could tell from the look in his eyes that he was from the streets. *I bet that nigga strapped too.* That fact immediately put Blaze at a disadvantage. *All niggas about nowadays is that damn gunplay.*

"My bad," Ghost shrugged, his smirk not matching his apology. He turned his attention back to Shantreis. "If that's all you got then we need to get more. You can gimme what you got now, though."

"Oh yeah," she answered nervously. As she bent down inside the car to retrieve her purse, Ghost's eyes were glued to her ass. He didn't even bother to be discreet about it.

"I got it, bruh," Blaze offered, reaching for the pump. It was probably foolish, but he pushed Ghost slightly as he took control. "Oh. My bad." He said it the same insincere way Ghost had.

"You think you funny, huh?"

Blaze shrugged casually just as Shantreis called him over. "Here you go," she said, folding the cash up and placing it in his hand. She hoped Blaze couldn't see what they were doing because she had no doubt that he would try to interfere. *That's the last thing we need.*

"'Preciate it, shawty. Good lookin' out." Ghost looked at Blaze pointedly before smacking Shantreis on the ass, admiring how it jiggled in her skintight leggings. *How you like that shit?* Ghost thought as he placed the money in his pocket.

Before Blaze could check Ghost for the disrespect, a new voice stepped into the conversation.

"Delonte!!! Who the fuck is that bitch?!"

Ghost sucked his teeth when he saw his girlfriend approaching them. "Malaysia, go sit yo' ass in the car! I done told you 'bout questionin' me and shit! I don't wanna have to beat yo' ass tonight!"

"Nigga, I wish you would!" she shouted back, knowing it was an empty threat. She looked Shantreis up and down. "The fuck you up here talkin' to that busted ass bitch for anyway?"

Busted?! Shantreis thought incredulously. *My face may be a lil' messed up but I'm far from busted. I know her Nicki Minaj ghetto ass ain't talkin'!* She wasn't about to let anyone disrespect her.

"Bitch—" Shantreis started.

"Man, y'all shut the fuck up!" Ghost commanded. "Go get in the car!" He turned back to Shantreis. "I'll be right back. I'm a' ride wit' you."

"For what?!" The color drained from her face. *What the fuck is this nigga plottin'?* She grabbed Ghost's arm.

He looked at her like she was crazy until she removed her hold on him.

Shantreis stepped closer to him so Blaze couldn't hear their conversation. "It's an ATM inside, I think. I can get the money there."

Ghost shook his head. "Nah. Just wait for me."

"Who the fuck was that nigga?" Blaze asked as he looked at Ghost's retreating figure.

"Trouble. That's all he is." Shantreis let out a deep sigh. They had more important shit to discuss than Ghost. "You didn't see the trunk raise up?!" She lowered her voice. "Outlaw is still alive! Why didn't you tie his ass up?!"

"Shit. I thought the nigga was dead. You saw him!"

Shantreis rolled her eyes. "You should've checked for a pulse, Blaze. What sense does that make? What if I had been driving and the police would've seen the shit?"

"That's why I came over here. Your right taillight is out... We should go back to the house."

"What?" she asked incredulously. "And do what?"

Blaze shrugged. "Leave that nigga body there, what else?"

"What the hell? If you thought we should just leave him at the house then why didn't you say so earlier?!" Shantreis hissed. "Now I gotta worry about Ghost." She was positive he wouldn't tell Cash. Hell, Cash wanted him dead anyway. He was the last person Shantreis thought he would talk to. Still, she had a nagging feeling that Ghost might have something else in mind.

"Because you wanted to be the fuckin' boss," Blaze pointed out, "It makes no fuckin' sense to drive around with a body in your trunk for an hour!"

Shantreis sighed. "Blaze, I swear to God!" She took a seat dejectedly. She was exhausted and just wanted to sleep. On top of that, her stomach was growling. *I just want this shit to be over with.* "Fine. Let's do it your way then."

Blaze nodded. "After we do, call up Cash and tell him Ghost did it."

"Nigga, are you crazy? I ain't gonna tell him that!"

"Why not? It'll get that nigga off your back. You know we can't trust that nigga either! If Cash is anything like Outlaw he'll probably shoot first and questions later. I bet he got some type of cleanup crew. We wouldn't have to worry about the shit no more."

"Nah, nah." Shantreis shook her head. "That shit could backfire too easily. I'll just say I don't know who did it." She cleared her throat. "I gotta take Ghost to the bank real quick."

"For what? His ol' lady got a car..." A knowing look washed over his face. "You scared of that nigga?"

Shantreis was quiet. "Just don't get involved. You don't know that nigga like I do. He'll pull a gun out on you in public and still pull the trigger. Lil' nigga crazy as hell!" She lowered her eyes and cleared her throat. "Go back to the car and just follow us, okay? Don't be too obvious though."

Blaze shook his head. "I can't believe this shit." He eyed Ghost suspiciously as he made his way back to Shantreis's car. He didn't agree with how she was going about things but he would listen this time. Resigned, he headed back to his own car.

"How you been?" Ghost greeted Shantreis like they hadn't just spoken a few minutes ago. He took a seat and reclined his chair, making himself comfortable.

"Good," she replied dryly as she placed the car in drive. "I'll go to the bank on the corner of Capital Boulevard and Spring Forest. My daily limit is five thousand though."

"Nah. Fuck that. That ain't enough but I bet you already knew that." Ghost grinned before pulling out his gun and pointing it at her. "Take me back to Outlaw's house. Gimme every fuckin' penny he got."

I need that damn money! She was alarmed at the thought of going back to being broke. "But—"

"Bitch, you can't hear?" To emphasize his point, Ghost placed the gun directly at her head. "Don't make me have to kill yo' ass cuz you know I will, right?"

Chapter 9

"Shantreis, don't try no dumb shit, a'ight?" Ghost advised.

"Ghost, you know I'm pregnant, right?" Shantreis repeated. She had already led him to the main safe. It was hidden in the stairs leading down to their basement. Now she was filling up a black trash bag with everything inside. She estimated there was at least sixty thousand dollars in here.

I remembered there being more in here, she thought. *Outlaw must've been moving the money around.* The safe upstairs in their bedroom probably only held about fifteen thousand, but it was better than nothing. It was Shantreis's plan to keep that for herself at least. She'd thought about bringing Ghost there instead, but figured it best not to try and humor him. He would know that was bullshit.

"So fuckin' what?" he asked, perplexed by the information she'd volunteered. "Oh…" A knowing look passed over his face. "You think I'm a' kill you or some shit?"

Hell yeah, she thought. *You said it first!*

Ghost chuckled, amused by her fear. "Do everything I say and you won't have shit to worry about."

Somehow the tone of his voice didn't soothe Shantreis's fears. *Ghost is the last nigga I should trust...*

"That's it?" he asked incredulously, noticing she was almost finished filling the bag.

"Yeah. Outlaw must've moved some of it... We got robbed a while back." Her voice shook nervously.

"Nah. This ain't all y'all muh'fuckas got!" Ghost yelled. Sixty stacks was the most money at one time he'd had in a while, but he figured Outlaw would have more than that. *Ain't no fuckin' way! Who this bitch tryna fool?*

Without forewarning, he fired a shot at the staircase. "Where the fuck is the rest of the money?!"

"Believe me!" she screamed. "This is it. We got maybe twenty thousand in our bedroom safe, but that's all!"

"Get up and gimme that, too!" Ghost barked. "Hurry the fuck up!" He kicked her butt swiftly, not hard enough to make her trip but enough that she lost her footing slightly.

Shantreis scurried up the stairs towards their bedroom. It was still trashed from the other day. Outlaw hadn't done anything to clean up. It didn't even look like he'd slept there the night before. She walked into the expansive walk-in closet.

Ghost looked around curiously. "Damn... What the fuck happened?" he bristled. "This where you killed that nigga at?"

"I didn't kill him," she lied.

"If it weren't you then it was that nigga you was with." Ghost shrugged. "Yo' co-defendant. Same fuckin' thing."

Shantreis was silent as she finished loading up the bag with the money. "There you go. It should be about eighty five thousand total."

Ghost grinned wickedly at the contents of the bag. The rich smell of the dirty money was intoxicating. He already had plans for it. "Nice doin' business wit' ya. 'Preciate it."

She nodded, backing away from him. She hoped he would keep his promise and leave.

"Close ya eyes," he instructed. "I'm a' go easy on you since you pregnant. Just count backwards from a hundred."

"Really?" Shantreis questioned gratefully.

"Yeah." Ghost nodded. Don't forget what I told ya ass earlier, either." He was sparing her only because he had plans for her later. Although some of the things he did didn't make sense to most people, there was a method to his madness. "Go ahead," he urged.

"A hundred... ninety-nine... ninety-eight..."

Ghost backed out, keeping his gun trained on her. He paused at the doorway for a moment, staring at Shantreis intently. He wanted to ensure she was following his directions to a tee. By the time she'd reached seventy, he felt satisfied enough to leave.

"Shantreis! Treis!" Blaze yelled as he entered the house.

As soon as he saw Ghost exit the house and get into the Benz with the girl from the gas station, he made his way over. Blaze had followed them carefully, only marginally surprised to see they'd doubled back to Outlaw's house. He'd parked down the street, waiting for Ghost to leave. It had taken everything in him not to go inside sooner, but he decided to heed Shantreis's advice. After all, Blaze didn't have a gun so that would put him at an immediate disadvantage.

Please be okay, he thought after she didn't respond. "Treis! Shantreis!"

Hearing a muffled voice coming in the direction of the garage, Blaze hurried over. Opening the door, he saw Shantreis struggling to pull Outlaw's lifeless body out of the trunk.

"Let me do that! Didn't the doctor tell you to take it easy?!" Blaze chided, gently pushing her out of the way. Effortlessly he carried Outlaw out. "You straight? That nigga didn't put his hands on you, did he?"

Shantreis shook her head. "Nah. I'm good. I just really wanna go home."

Knock knock knock!

Shantreis and Blaze looked over at each other panic-stricken. The knocking was so loud it resembled the police.

Fuck! Shantreis thought. *Did Ghost call the police on us? Bitch ass nigga. I should've known somethin' was up. He let me off too easy. Or is it the fuckin' FEDS?* She silently said a prayer. Shantreis always knew the day could come, but she'd hoped Outlaw would be out of the game before then.

"Go see who it is," Blaze hissed, stopping in the doorway.

"Shouldn't we run?" she questioned. "Ain't they just gonna come in anyway?"

"Now who scary?" he mimicked her earlier words to him. "Go!"

Cautiously she approached the door, just as the pounding sounded again.

"Ay, Outlaw?! Shantreis?! Y'all home?"

Shit! She didn't even have to look through the peephole to know it was Cash standing on the other side. Noticing Blaze had left the door unlocked, she quickly locked it before running back to Blaze.

"It's Cash!" she whispered loudly. "Put Outlaw back where he was in the living room! Then you go out the back door." Another thought quickly crossed her mind. "Do you think he saw you?"

"Nah…" Blaze said, but the faltering of his voice gave away his uncertainty. *He didn't, right?*

Fuck it, she thought. *Either way he'll be gone before Cash comes in.* Shantreis sucked in a deep breath. It was time for her to put on her best act for Cash. He wouldn't be easy to deceive so she had to make it believable. Running to the kitchen sink, she splashed water onto a dish towel. Roughly she scrubbed her face in an attempt to remove the makeup. Shantreis's bruises were still fresh and would be just enough to help sell her story.

Just in case, she thought, looking around the kitchen until she found what she was looking for. She picked up a small steak knife from the butcher's block. Drawing in a deep breath, she brought it to her throat creating a small laceration.

"I'm a' text you the address to my new place. Come over when you done," Blaze told her before disappearing out the back door.

Shantreis nodded. She could hear Outlaw's phone going off again. It was probably Cash calling. The knocking had ceased, but a quick glance out the window revealed his Bentley was still in the driveway.

"Cash!" she shouted hysterically with tears in her eyes as she opened the door. "Help me! They killed him! They killed Outlaw!"

"What?" Cash asked in disbelief, pushing past Shantreis into the house. When he saw his nigga laid out on the floor, he paused. Shantreis was explaining but he was only half-listening. The only thing on his mind was the fact that the nigga he'd considered a brother was dead.

Cash turned to face her abruptly. "Do you know who did it? Did you see their faces? How many niggas was it?"

Shantreis hesitated, placing a hand on her forehead. She was pretending like she was hurting, but she was actually stalling. "It was two niggas. They had masks on so their voices were muffled."

He grabbed her by the shoulders, seeking answers in her eyes. "I really need you to think, Shantreis. Try to remember every fuckin' detail about them muthafuckas!" Cash roared. "Did any of them niggas resemble Ghost?!"

"Uh... I-It..." Ghost's name sat on the tip of her tongue, remembering Blaze's earlier suggestion. She knew very well of the bad blood between the brothers. Shantreis also knew how close Cash and Outlaw were. If she threw Ghost under the bus, she had no doubt Cash would kill him regardless of any excuse he could give—even if he tried to put the blame back on her.

"On his left hand, he got a tattoo that makes it look like you can see his bones," Cash tried to jog her memory.

Why the fuck would he believe Ghost? Shantreis's thoughts continued. *Blaze is right. This is probably the best way.*

After about thirty seconds of silently weighing out the pros and cons, she finally gave her answer.

Chapter 10

"Oh my God, Travaris! Noooo!!!"

Shantreis rolled her eyes at the scene Kaleesha was making at Outlaw's funeral. She was glad the black veil she wore covered most of her face so no one could see her true thoughts. *She's crying more than the baby,* she thought, glancing over at Monet.

The child cried silently but her heartbreaking facial expression spoke louder than anything else. She clung tightly to the small pink elephant Outlaw had bought her when she was born. Her name was embroidered on the floppy ear.

Shantreis diverted her attention away from Monet and scanned the rest of the church. It was filled with hundreds of spectators dressed in black, mourning over Outlaw's death. She was certain only a few knew him on a personal level.

Probably just the bitches he cheated on me with and the niggas he worked with, she thought. Everyone else gave off the impression they were at a fashion show or the club. Shantreis expected it seeing as every hood celebrity in Raleigh—from the dope boys to the local rappers were in attendance. This was definitely the place to find a baller.

Her eyes moved back to the front of the giant church. A gold-plated coffin rested front and center with a picture of Outlaw next to it. The preacher was going on about something but Shantreis couldn't hear him.

"They took away my baby's father! My baby ain't got no daddy no more!" Kaleesha's hysterics continued, drowning out any other sounds.

Fallon sat to Shantreis's right, squeezing her hand tightly. Her eyes were wet with tears.

Shantreis found it ironic. She had been with Outlaw for over three years. Even still she couldn't bring herself to shed any tears for him. Looking at his casket made her feel slightly guilty, but it was an emotion that never lasted long. The nightmares she had daily proved otherwise, however.

Could this have been avoided? Shantreis wondered briefly before shaking her head. *Fuck all that would've, could've, should've. It's too late now. Besides, I know damn good and well if I hadn't gotten him, he would've gotten me.*

Cash sat on a pew on the opposite side. He appeared unaffected, but she knew differently.

What if he finds out it was me? Shantreis thought. She couldn't find the courage to blame it on Ghost so she simply told him she didn't know. Losing her money still had her pissed, but staying with Blaze in his new condo at The Dawson somewhat made up for it. He'd made good use of his money. In addition to his condo, he'd purchased a new pitch black Audi A7.

For some quick cash, Shantreis sold Outlaw's Maserati. Now she had a good fifty stacks lining her pockets. *I should make a couple more stacks after the garage sale, too. Shit. Fuck the garage sale, when the townhouse sells I really won't be hurtin' for sure.* She wasted no time placing their townhome on the market and planned on selling everything inside of it as well. All she could see was dollar signs.

"His mother has a few words," the preacher said. "Ms. Robinson." He motioned towards the podium.

Shantreis raised her eyebrow. She hadn't seen his mom in quite a while. Ms. Robinson was a short, stout woman with coffee colored skin. She reminded Shantreis of the actress Loretta Devine. She didn't associate much with her son, only dropping in to borrow money here and there. She'd left Outlaw with his late grandmother while she chased whatever man showed her a bit of attention.

His momma wasn't shit then and ain't shit now, she thought. *And she got the nerve to come here and speak. She never came when he was alive.*

"Thank you all for taking the time to come out and celebrate the life of my son Travaris…" Ms. Robinson started. She was still speaking but Shantreis tuned her out.

"Wake me up when it's over," she whispered to Fallon. She didn't wait for a reply before closing her eyes.

"Are you okay?" Fallon prodded Cash as the funeral let out.

"Yeah I'm good," he replied curtly.

"I haven't heard from you since we first talked about the baby." She struggled to keep up with his quick pace. Fallon knew he was trying to avoid her but she wouldn't be deterred.

"Well now you realize why." Cash paused momentarily to look at her. "I hope you know that now isn't the right time to continue the conversation either."

"Then when, Damontrez? I can never get a hold of you."

"They just put my nigga in the ground. I been knowin' him since... Hell, since before I even knew about my real brothers." Cash grabbed her arm, leading her away from the crowd of people. "Don't do this here, Fallon. I'll talk to you later."

"I just want to know about you and Remy." Fallon spotted her earlier, but she didn't think she came with Cash. "And what you were telling me before... you said—"

"Fallon, let me explain somethin' to you." Cash furrowed his eyebrows. "The shit honestly ain't none of your damn business. On top of that, you couldn't have waited?"

Fallon was quiet. "I'm sorry. I just—"

"Man, I'll holla at you later." His voice was full of exasperation as he waved her off like a mosquito.

"So what the fuck is up?" Ghost asked his brother. They were sitting inside of his new Dodge Challenger. Ghost wasted no time spending some of the money he'd stolen.

"Fallon's pregnant," Strap informed.

"Damn... Is it—?"

"Yeah. It's Cash's baby."

"Damn, bruh." He stopped at the light on the intersection of Martin Luther King Jr. Boulevard and State Road. They'd just left their weedman's house. It was nearing midnight and the roads were deserted. He placed the car into park so he could finish rolling his blunt.

"You'll be that lil' nigga uncle and his stepdaddy." Ghost shook his head. His facial expression was solemn but his voice was playful. *That's fucked up though,* he thought.

"It is what it is," Strap said good-humoredly, not letting his brother's words get to him. He rolled down his window slightly, inviting the light sprinkle of rain to come inside the car. It was an unconventional situation but what could he do? He wanted Fallon. If he wanted her, he knew he had to accept all of her.

"I don't know what the fuck type shit you on." He grunted. "And didn't you say that bitch still wearin' that nigga ring?"

"Nigga, just roll the blunt." Strap gazed out the tinted window in an attempt to avoid the question. He honestly couldn't remember if she'd had it on last time. *That damn pregnancy test threw me off.*

"Sucka for love ass nigga," Ghost mumbled.

"Help! Help me!!"

"What the fuck?!" they cursed in unison.

A woman was running in their direction. It looked like she'd come out of the woods. Her hair was wild and her makeup was streaked over her tear-stained face. Clad only in lingerie and a pair of heels, she carried clothes in her hands. Noticing their car, she rushed over to it, pounding on the doors and pulling the door handles. Unfortunately for her, all the doors were locked.

"Please help!!!" she pleaded, noticing the small crack in Strap's window. "He tried to rape me!"

Strap looked over at Ghost. "You ain't gon' let her in?"

"Hell nah. I don't know that bitch." Ghost placed his .45 on his lap as he put the car in gear. "I ain't fallin' for the okey doke. This could be a set up or some shit. She got the right muthafuckin' one though."

"Yo' scary ass." Strap looked at the girl again, studying her closely. "Shit. Hold up. That's Taeja."

"Hell nah!" Ghost's face lit up with glee. "What the fuck type of shit is this bitch into?"

"I don't know but I can't leave her out there like that." Strap tugged on the lock, opening the door. "C'mon, sweetheart." He appeared at her side, draping his jacket over her shoulders to cover her exposed skin.

Taeja's body was shaking frantically as Strap ushered her into the backseat. He took a seat next to her.

Ghost watched her from the rearview mirror, focusing on her ample cleavage. "You wanna hit the blunt? It'll calm you down."

"No, thank you," she answered, gazing blankly out the window as they pulled off.

"You said you got raped?" Ghost asked. "Where that nigga at?" There were a few houses around but he couldn't tell which one she'd come from.

"Chill out, Ghost," Strap spoke up. He knew she would talk about it when she was ready.

Taeja unfolded the clothes in her hands and put them on. Normally she would have felt uncomfortable, but they'd seen everything already anyway. Still, she noticed Strap was respectful enough to look away. Ghost's eyes kept meeting hers, however.

"You gonna be okay?" Strap asked after she'd finished.

Taeja ran a hand through her tangled hair. "I'm doing dumb shit just like 'Nessa! I knew better!" Hot tears stung her face. "I can't believe that nigga tried to rape me!"

"You safe now," Strap soothed her, placing a comforting arm around her shoulder. "It's okay."

"I-I just needed money to pay my bills because my hours got cut. If I don't make the money by Friday then we're going to get evicted. This dude that comes in the store a lot named Chauncey used to give me money sometimes." Taeja sniffled. "He told me he got me. He would give me the money but he said I had to come over and get it.

"He said he'd give me two thousand dollars. I didn't have enough money to get my car out of the shop so I rode a taxi here."

"You really thought that nigga was gonna give you two stacks for free?" Ghost snorted in disbelief. *Bitches nowadays.* "You know that nigga thought he was gettin' some pussy."

"Ghost, shut the fuck up, man." Strap shook his head. *This nigga so insensitive.*

"He said he didn't want anything in return," Taeja insisted, her voice taking on a hardened tone. She already felt naïve. The last person she wanted to rub it in was Ghost. "I managed to kick him in the balls with my shoe."

"Damn," Strap muttered under his breath. She was wearing four-inch heels that had decorative spikes on the toe.

"So I ran out before he raped me but he knows where I work… I'm afraid he's going to try to do something to me."

"Don't worry about it," Strap assured her. "I got you. Let me know the next time you work. I'll make sure that nigga won't fuck with you."

Oh yeah? Ghost thought, raising an eyebrow. *This nigga here... Captain Save-A-Ho.*

"No," she said quickly. "I couldn't ask you to do that..."

"Nah. I *want* to," he persisted.

"Really?" Strap nodded and she returned a gracious smile. "Thank you, Damien. I'm really grateful."

The rest of the ride to Taeja's house was void of conversation. Old school Biggie Smalls 'Ready to Die' pumped from the speakers as background music. Strap stole a few looks at Taeja each time the streetlights flashed across her face. Despite her disheveled appearance, he still found her attractive.

What the fuck? Strap's thoughts were betraying him. He'd just been thinking about Fallon and their future earlier that day. So why was he looking at Taeja this way? *Probably just because I feel bad for her. Yeah. That's it.* Feeling satisfied with his reasoning, he turned away from her.

Ghost pulled into her complex several minutes later, following Taeja's directions. "Right here?"

"Yes. Thank you," Taeja said as she opened the car door. "For everything."

"No problem." Strap got out as well so he could sit in the front seat, but her earlier words echoed in his mind. "Ay, Taeja!" When she turned around, he placed twenty crisp hundred dollar bills into the palm of her hand.

"What? Why?" She looked down at the money, taken aback by his gesture. "I can't take this from you."

"You can't save your ass and your pride at the same time," Strap lectured with a smile.

"But this is too much—"

"It's what you needed, right?"

"Right," she said softly. "I'll pay you back..." Taeja's eyes suddenly narrowed, recalling the night's prior events. "Or is there something else you wanted?"

Strap looked at her confused. "What?"

"I don't believe you're giving me this for nothing. What do you want from me?"

"I don't want shit from you." He was offended and didn't hide it. "I just wanted to help you out. I was raised by a single mother so I know the struggle. Shit. If someone had been in me and my brother's lives," he nodded towards Ghost, "like this then it probably wouldn't have turned out the way it is now."

"I guess..." she mumbled, still not completely convinced. Reluctantly she placed the money into the pocket of her jeans.

"Your little girl—your niece—needs you. If you don't take it, then how are you gonna get the money? You want a repeat of tonight?" There was no trace of humor in his voice. It may have sounded harsh but he needed to drill it in her head.

"I'll pay you back," Taeja promised. "A friend of mine will be hooking me up with a job soon so I can put my degree to use."

"I told you I didn't want anything—"

"If you won't, I'm not gonna accept it," she countered with a mischievous grin.

Strap cracked a smile. "Your lil' ass is real stubborn." He pulled a dollar bill out of his pocket and wrote his number on it. "Hit me up. Let me know when you have to work."

"Thank you for everything." She knelt down over the car so Ghost could see her face. "Thank you, D."

Strap watched her as she entered her building. His gaze lingered a little longer than it should have.

Chapter 11

"When does your lease end?" Strap asked Fallon as he reclined on her canopy bed.

Strap had just arrived a few minutes ago. Fallon was already getting ready for bed, flitting around the bathroom doing her nightly routine. She managed to turn him on even when she had that ridiculous headscarf on and a plain, oversized T-shirt. The fact that it was *his* shirt she was wearing made it even sexier. It swallowed her diminutive frame, but still her soft curves could be found. His manhood swelled as he watched her. Besides a few quick smooches and cuddling, they hadn't done anything since the day Cash had walked in on them.

"In a couple of months," Fallon replied, looking at him curiously. "Why do you ask?"

"Cuz your apartment is a one bedroom." Strap cleared his throat, forcing himself to refocus on the conversation at hand. "We're gonna need more space with the baby."

Fallon nodded her head in agreement. "You're right."

"So… I was thinkin' we should start lookin' for a house. I'm tired of driving all the way over here from Zebulon."

"A house?" she asked with surprise, lying down beside him. "For us? Are you serious?"

"Yeah. It don't make no sense to keep throwin' money at an apartment when we can actually own something and build equity."

Fallon smiled, impressed by him. "You've been really looking into it and thinking about it, huh?"

Strap nodded as he took off his shirt. "I been thinkin' about a lot of shit. I looked into enrolling at Shaw too…" His eyes traveled to her ring finger. *Are you fuckin' kiddin' me?*

"You don't think we're rushing this though?" she asked.

"Shit. We might be…" He nodded at the engagement ring. "Why you still wearin' it?"

Embarrassed, Fallon looked down at her finger before placing her hands behind her back. "It's just a habit… It's not a big deal."

Strap raised an eyebrow. "You sure?"

"What are you trying to say, Damien?" she questioned, matching his accusatory tone.

He shrugged. "I'm just wonderin' what's the *real* reason you still wearin' another nigga ring?"

"Are you insecure or something? I'm trying to tell you it's nothing like that." Reluctantly she removed the ring and placed it in her nightstand's drawer.

"It ain't about bein' insecure, Fallon. It's about the shit bein' disrespectful." He shrugged. "I don't know why you still got it anyway."

Fallon sighed. "I don't wanna argue with you, Strap." *Because I might say something I'll regret,* she thought. "The ring is off." She flicked off the light switch before hopping into bed and turning her back to him. "Good night."

"Yup," Strap said dully. He was no fool. He was aware there was more to it than Fallon was letting on. *Shit ain't nothing like I thought it would be...*

"Man, it feels like forever since we've gotten up," Shantreis commented as she and Fallon strolled into Babies 'R Us. In all actuality only a week had passed since Outlaw's funeral, but the girls had barely spoken on the phone so it seemed much longer.

"I was trying to give you time to grieve," Fallon admitted.

Shantreis crinkled her nose. "Girl, I'm good. I do *not* think about that nigga."

Fallon smiled. "I bet. Your world revolves around Blaze now," she teased.

Shantreis returned the smile, not bothering to deny Fallon's playful allegation. It was true. She and Blaze were getting along well. In fact, it made her regret not hooking up with him sooner.

"Did you know Cash is fucking with Remy?" Fallon asked abruptly. She'd noticed a girl in the baby superstore that reminded her of Remy and couldn't help bringing it back up.

"Nah. But I'm not surprised."

Fallon narrowed her eyebrows, wondering what Shantreis knew that she didn't. "Why do you say that?"

"Because they were fuckin' with each other for a while," Shantreis responded nonchalantly before walking over to the baby registry table.

Fallon waited for her friend impatiently as the associate explained the process to her. *So she knows they got history? But she didn't tell me?*

"This shit is so cute," Shantreis gushed as she took the registry gun in hand and zapped a Winnie the Pooh robe.

"What do you mean? You knew about it but you didn't tell me?"

Shantreis spun around quickly with a grimace. "Fallon, what are you talkin' about? You knew too but you didn't care, remember? I told you that Cash and Remy was talkin'… Matter fact, the first day you went out with him! When I told you, you brushed that shit off." She imitated her friend's voice, "You said 'If she's not his official girlfriend then it doesn't matter. If they were together, he wouldn't be going out with me.' Remember?"

Fallon was quiet. She *did* remember that. *I can't believe that was Remy. Wow. I guess I did kinda steal Cash from her.* "Well, it was four years ago when I said that." She was embarrassed by what she'd said back then. "I don't understand why she's back in the picture now."

"I mean, she was his baby momma. You know how niggas is."

"Baby momma?" Fallon looked at her incredulously. "That bitch got an abortion. That don't count."

Fallon missed the knowing expression on Shantreis's face as she continued to rifle through baby things. If she had seen it, she would have definitely known there was more to the story than her friend was letting on.

"Yeah," Shantreis said finally. "They kept fuckin' around again after y'all broke up too. Nothin' serious though."

"That day when we first ran into Ghost and Strap, I *asked* you if he was seeing anybody and you said 'no'!" Fallon insisted, feeling like a homewrecker for the second time in a row.

"Like I said, she was irrelevant. *You're* the one he has tatted on him, Fallon. He put you as wifey. Remy is irrelevant. I think Cash fucks with her out of convenience, not because he has feelings for the bitch." Shantreis stared at her friend. "Why you asking about Cash all of a sudden? I thought you and Strap were together?"

"We are. I was just wondering because when I told Cash I was pregnant—"

"Bitch!" Shantreis practically screamed. "Why the fuck am I just now hearin' about it?!" She shook her head. "Damn. You had all this time to tell me and you didn't! When are you due?!"

Fallon looked to the floor in shame. "I didn't tell you because I'm not sure. I did something real dumb… I want your advice." She lifted her head, making eye contact with Shantreis. "Don't judge me though."

"Go ahead."

She sucked in a deep breath and lowered her voice. "I went and bought a pregnancy test but the results were negative. I thought it was impossible since I had morning sickness…"

"Okay…." Shantreis said, wondering where the story was going. "So what? The tests are wrong sometimes. Like if it's too early or if you bought one of them cheap shits from the dollar store."

"No! That's not it… After Cash caught us, I really *really* wanted him back. Me and Strap had gotten into it too so I felt like I had do something…"

Shantreis's eyes widened. *I know this bitch ain't gonna say what I think.* "What did you do, Fallon?!"

"I went on Craig's List and bought a positive pregnancy test so I could show Cash," she admitted. "I figured a baby might make him forgive me sooner and bring us closer."

"Fallon, what the fuck? Are you stupid?" Shantreis shook her head. "What are you gonna tell him when there's no baby?!"

"I just know I'm pregnant, Treis! I *have* to be! I haven't had my period in a while either!" Fallon argued weakly. She'd believed that initially, but after reading the side effects to one of the medications she was taking, she doubted it more and more. Vomiting was one of the side effects. She wondered if her "morning sickness" was due to that.

"I scheduled a doctor's appointment so I'll know soon enough. I'm too scared to buy another test, just in case it's negative."

"Fallon, that was dumb as hell. What you gonna do— fake a miscarriage if you find out you was wrong?"

"If I have to," she admitted.

"I knew you was scandalous," a new voice joined their conversation.

"Excuse you," Fallon started, but when she turned around, she wished she hadn't. "Remy… What are you doing here?"

Remy stood there with a smug expression on her face. "I didn't believe I needed your permission to go shopping."

"Why the hell were you eavesdropping?" Shantreis asked, shaking her head. *Some people are too damn nosy.*

"Cuz I can," she replied childishly. "You can bet I'm gonna tell Cash what you said, too."

"Like Cash will believe you!" Fallon scoffed.

"Oh he will," she assured. "I ain't never lied to him, but it's cool cuz I got proof anyway." She held up her iPhone and motioned towards the ear buds in her ears. "I recorded the whole damn conversation. I'm gonna send it to him, too."

Without thinking, Fallon lunged at Remy, pulling at her long tresses savagely. "Bitch! Gimme that fuckin' phone!"

"Are you fuckin' crazy?!" Remy screamed trying to get away. Fallon was petite, but she had more strength than anticipated.

Fallon wildly yanked Remy until they were both on the floor. Both girls had grabbed each other's hair cursing out the other to let go.

Shantreis laughed as she watched. She loved her friend, but she couldn't fight for shit. *She still beating Remy ass though.* Noticing Remy had dropped her phone, Shantreis picked it up and stuffed it into her purse inconspicuously.

"Someone call security!" another customer's voice called out. "Get help!"

Shit, Shantreis thought. "Let go, Remy! Let go!" she shouted, prying her fingers out of Fallon's hair. "I said let go, bitch!" Shantreis smacked her in the face, catching the girl off guard. She held out a hand to her friend, helping her up. The two girls ran out of the store like they stole something.

The moment they entered Fallon's car, they both erupted into laughter. "Girl, you goofy as hell!" Shantreis handed over Remy's cell phone. "Here."

"Thank you. I can't let her tell Cash! He already thinks I'm a liar. I want to tell him myself... just not now."

Shantreis turned to her seriously. "Does it matter anymore though, Fallon? You're happy with Strap right?"

"Yeah but—"

"Then Cash's opinion should be irrelevant. Since him and Strap got bad blood, it ain't like you'd ever have to fuck with the nigga again. Raleigh's big enough. You wouldn't have to see him."

She has a point, Fallon thought, but she couldn't stop how she felt. Although their relationship was over, she still didn't want to give him any more reason to dislike her, even if it was deserved. *Who wants to look bad in front of someone anyway?*

Fallon opened her car door and put Remy's phone behind her tire. *I can't stop her from telling him, but at the end of the day, it's my word against hers.* Placing her BMW in reverse, she smiled as she heard the crunch of the phone. *Mission accomplished.*

Fallon continued out of the parking space, but was forced to stop when Remy stood directly in her path. She blared her horn and rolled down her window. "Move out the way, Remy, before I beat your ass again!"

"Where's my fuckin' phone?! Gimme my damn phone!"

Fallon laughed. "We don't have it. Sorry!"

Remy nodded her head with a knowing smirk. She walked towards Fallon's door. "I don't know what the fuck y'all did with my fuckin' phone but it don't even matter!"

She chuckled. "I already sent the shit when we were in the store. Joke's on you, bitch!"

Chapter 12

Fallon gazed at her cell phone uneasily. It had been two days since her run in with Remy. Surprisingly, she hadn't heard from Cash. *Was Remy bluffing?* Fallon had been waiting for the call that would undoubtedly come, with Cash cursing her out and calling her everything but a child of God. *Or maybe he's not calling since he said he didn't want to have anything to do with me anyway. Oh well.* She turned her attention towards the big bay windows in her living room.

It was a beautiful day outside, a stark contrast from the rainy weather Raleigh had been having lately. Fallon and Shantreis were supposed to go check out a new restaurant that just opened up downtown called Grandma Chick's. From what she'd heard, it was reminiscent of Gladys Knight's Chicken & Waffles in Atlanta. The only problem was Shantreis called and cancelled earlier since Blaze had the day off at work.

I'm hungry now. Heck, I'm already dressed. Unlike most, Fallon didn't mind eating out alone. She was comfortable in her own company. *I'm tired of being cooped up in the house.*

Fallon grabbed her ostrich leather Prada tote off the kitchen island and headed for the door. As she pulled her keys to lock the door, she heard her ringtone going off.

Thought we'd stay together, always and forever... But now I see that no one is inseparable...

Recognizing it immediately, Fallon froze.

It was Cash.

What should I do? she wondered. Her finger hovered over 'Decline' but she surprised herself when she hit 'Accept' instead. "Hello?"

"Hey. What's up? You busy?"

"No..." Fallon answered cautiously.

"I wanted to come over and talk to you... about everything," Cash said earnestly. "You home?"

Yes... But instead she said, "No. I'm actually on my way to Grandma Chick's."

There was a slight pause, then, "You and Strap?"

Fallon felt like she detected a slight bit of jealousy in his voice. "No. Just me."

"You mind if I join you then?"

She couldn't help the smile that slowly spread across her face. "Really?" She was surprised by his request.

"Yeah. I'll meet you there."

"Okay. Bye." Just as soon as Fallon disconnected the call, she saw Strap's name appear her on her caller ID.

Damn. First Cash and now Strap? she thought of the coincidence.

"Hey, Strap," she greeted.

"Whassup, baby? Whatchu doin'?"

"About to leave the house. Headed out to eat."

"With Shantreis?"

"Yeah." The lie rolled off Fallon's tongue unconsciously. *Why am I lying to him?* So far she'd been truthful with Strap each time Cash spoke to her, but now she felt like she couldn't say.

"Damn. I wanted to take you out to eat."

"We could still do dinner," she offered.

"A'ight, baby. I'll holla at you later then."

Strap disconnected the call. He was already in Raleigh, only about ten minutes away from where Fallon lived.

"It's nice that y'all reconciled," Taeja spoke up. She was riding shotgun. Strap had just picked her up from work, as promised.

"Yeah." He grinned. "Thanks to you."

"Oh yeah?" She forced a smile. Although she'd encouraged him before, now she wished they *had* broken up. It was true that Taeja didn't know much about Strap but from what he'd shown her, he was a gentleman. There weren't many men in the world like him. If there were, she had never met one until now. Most of the men she knew acted like Ghost.

"Yeah. Maybe y'all could meet some day. You kinda remind me of her."

I doubt it, Taeja thought confidently. "How so?" she asked instead. She couldn't picture what kind of girl he would date but she didn't want to either.

"Both of y'all are smart and innocent... Is that the word?" Strap waved his hand trying to jog his memory but he couldn't find the word he was looking for. "I don't know but y'all are different. Good girls who grew up in the suburbs... Y'all don't know shit about the street life."

"And you do?" she asked curiously.

Taeja could tell Strap had some hood in him, although he'd never elaborated much about himself. She knew he would be attending Shaw University next semester. The Charger SRT8 he drove wasn't overly flashy either like most street niggas she knew of. He didn't strike her as a dope boy, especially not with his more tailored and preppy style of dress. He wasn't parading around in skinny jeans, but he wasn't dressed like a rapper from the early 2000s either. Strap's swag was his own and he made it look damn good.

Strap shrugged as he looked over at her. "I used to but I ain't 'bout that life no more. Had to grow up, you know? Me and my girl got a baby on the way so I can't be caught up with that kinda shit."

A baby? Taeja thought. *Damn… They're pretty much a family.* "Oh" was all she could manage. She returned her attention out the window, no longer in the mood to talk.

Strap noticed her withdrawal but had no clue what was wrong with her. "You straight? You not still thinkin' about that shit with that nigga, right?"

He glanced over at her, his pretty brown eyes appearing lighter from the way the sun hit them. *Them lashes though,* Taeja thought in mock envy. His eyelashes were longer than hers. "No. I'm good." She turned away from him quickly, worried he'd catch her staring. In five minutes they'd reached her apartment complex.

"Thanks for the ride, Damien," she said when he pulled to a stop.

"No problem."

Taeja started to get out, but Strap grabbed her by the wrist gently, effectively stopping her. "Listen, you wanna go get somethin' to eat? I'm hungry as hell but I don't want fast food." Strap gave her another boyish grin. "I ain't tryna eat alone in a restaurant either."

"I don't have any money to—"

"It's on me," he spoke up quickly. "When you're with me, you don't have to worry about money, a'ight?"

The way he'd said it sent shivers down her spine but she tried to play it off. "I have to pick up Kairi so I don't think that…"

"She can come, too."

'What about your girlfriend?' was the next question Taeja wanted to pose, but why fake the funk? She didn't give a damn about her. They were just going out to eat. It was innocent. Friends could eat together, couldn't they?

"Okay. We'll go," she relented.

"When you come in, look to your right and you'll see me," Fallon instructed. She tried to glance out the French doors of the restaurant, but it was so crowded. It had only been open for a week so many residents of Wake County were still trying to check it out. Fallon had been waiting for fifteen minutes already. She'd been quoted a thirty minute time frame but she didn't mind. She'd needed time to get her thoughts together.

A smile came to her face when she saw Cash striding through the door. She stood up from her seat in the waiting area to meet him. "Hey. You actually came."

Cash looked at her surprised. "Yeah. I said I was." His eyes roamed around the packed restaurant. "Damn. I didn't know it was gonna be like this. I could barely find a park."

"I know," she agreed, nodding her head. "I think it will be worth it though." Fallon showed him the buzzer in her hand. "We have maybe fifteen minutes left."

He nodded. "So how you been feelin'? You havin' morning sickness or cravings?"

Is this a trick question? she wondered. Fallon searched his face but he seemed to be sincerely asking. "I'm much better. Why did you wanna see me?"

Cash sighed deeply before looking her directly in the eyes. "I been thinkin' a lot since Outlaw's funeral... Life's too short for the bullshit. We're gonna be in each other's lives for at least eighteen years. We need to get along."

"Yeah, you're right," Fallon agreed, feeling guilty as hell.

He looked up thoughtfully. "I'm gettin' a second shot at bein' a dad and I ain't gonna fuck it up this time."

Once again she felt like shit. Fallon was hurt that Remy had been his first but knowing he might not actually have the second chance he was looking for hurt more. *I can't even begin to imagine how much he's gonna hate me when he finds out the truth.*

"What really happened last year between me and Remy..." Cash looked around for a seat, knowing he wouldn't be able to stand up while he told this story. Locating one, he pulled Fallon after him. "She did get pregnant... but she didn't get an abortion, miscarry, or whatever else bullshit you were told."

Fallon's eyes widened. "Did she have the baby?" she near whispered.

He nodded his head solemnly.

"Where-Where was I?"

"At school, Fallon. Me and you were done when this happened. I mean, it's true I did fuck around and sleep with her while me and you was still together—that *is* how she got pregnant. I just didn't fuck with her again after I did that. I felt bad about it—"

"How could you cheat on me, Damontrez?" Fallon interrupted. It was one thing to have heard something she'd initially dismissed as a rumor, but another for him to confirm it as true. She knew she had no right to be mad. *Sleeping with Strap while I was with him was worse, I guess. But it's because he slept with Remy in the first place that all of this happened.* "Why?"

"You nagged me, Fallon, *a lot.*"

"And it gave you the right to cheat on me?"

"Hear me out." Cash put up a hand to quiet her. "It wasn't just that. You know we were going through a lot of shit around that time. You had school and I was knee deep in the game tryna make a name for myself. It was never my intention to sleep with that girl. It just happened. We was celebratin' Outlaw's birthday and she was there... Shit just happened," he explained.

The excuse sounded flimsy as hell to her. *This from the same man who told me you can't mistakenly sleep with someone.* "I'm just so shocked. I can't believe it."

"You could never be more shocked than I was to see my brother and girl sleeping together though," his voice hardened.

Point taken, she thought.

"I gotta deal with the fact you and my brother are gonna be together..." He gritted his teeth after the statement left his mouth.

Disappointment dripped from his words, or was it resentment? Fallon couldn't tell but knowing Cash, it was likely both.

"Anyway, Remy never aborted the baby. She had to be put on bedrest when she got to be 'bout five months... Then we had the baby. A girl. Her name was Niyah."

Fallon's breath caught in her throat. Her eyes were widened with surprise. She couldn't believe what she was hearing. *What happened to her? Has he been hiding his daughter too?*

"She was only a month old when she died," he said quietly.

Earlier he said it was his fault... The suspense was killing Fallon.

"After she was born, I moved Remy and Niyah to my house for a little bit. Niyah had everything but it was that fuckin' crib I bought..." Cash shook his head. "Her neck..." His voice trailed off as he took a second to recompose himself. "Her neck got stuck in a gap between the side rail and the headboard. It was my fault cuz I didn't notice there was a screw loose."

"Cash, I'm so sorry." She covered her mouth with her hands. Her eyes were watery just imagining the pain he was in. Reflexively she found herself hugging him as best she could due to the way they were seated. The couple sitting next to them had just gotten up, making it a bit easier for her to comfort him.

Outwardly Cash seemed fine, but Fallon knew him better than anybody. From the broken tone of his voice and the lost look in his eyes while he spoke, she knew he had a lot of inner turmoil. "I didn't know. But why didn't you share that with me before?"

He only shook his head in response. "I don't like to talk about it. Who the hell wants to think about how they failed as a fuckin' parent? How they killed their child?"

"Don't say that. It wasn't your fault, baby."

"Excuse me, but is anyone sitting here?" a voice cut in from nearby.

"No," Cash and Fallon said in unison.

"Hey, Fallon!"

Fallon turned her head slightly from its position on Cash's chest to over at the woman calling out to her. She mustered a smile, wiping at her moistened eyes. "Hey, Taeja. What are you doing here?"

"I'm just out to eat with a friend. But who is this? Your fiancé?" Taeja chattered excitedly. She looked from Cash back to Fallon. "You did a good job, girl! He's cute. Y'all make a cute couple."

"Fallon?" a familiar voice called.

What the fuck? Fallon thought when Strap headed in their direction with a baby carrier in hand. The beautiful little girl sitting in it eyed the scene in front of her with interest.

"This is my friend Damien," Taeja introduced, seemingly oblivious to the growing tension. "Damien, this is my old friend from college, Fallon and her fiancé…" Her voice trailed off. "I didn't catch your name. I'm sorry."

"I'm Cash," he announced with a smirk, "But she's not my fiancé… anymore."

Fallon straightened up quickly as Strap's eyes bore a hole through hers. Quickly, she removed her arms from around Cash. She was so surprised to see Strap that she had been unaware of the position she was still in and how it must have looked.

"She's *my* girlfriend," Strap corrected.

Chapter 13

"What?" Taeja looked at the three of them in confusion. "Fallon is your girlfriend?"

"Strap, what are you doing here?" Fallon asked, standing up just as the buzzer she was holding went off. Their table was ready but it was the last thing on her mind.

"Where's Shantreis?" he countered cynically.

"She couldn't make it. Why are you here with her?" Her eyes went to the baby and then to Taeja. "Looking like a happy little family…"

Fallon didn't care how her situation may have looked to Strap at this moment. The only thing on her mind was why Strap was eating out with some bitch with a baby. She wondered if he, too, had a secret child she knew nothing about. It occurred to her that she was probably being ridiculous but she was too pissed off to think straight.

Violently, Fallon threw the buzzer at Strap's chest. "Are you cheatin' on me with this bitch?!" Still vibrating, it clattered to the floor loudly. That sound combined with her now high-pitched voice had stolen the attention of most of the patrons.

"Fallon, you better chill the fuck out," Strap warned. If it was one thing he hated, it was causing a scene.

"No! Not until you tell me why you're here with her!"

"Believe me, Fallon," Taeja spoke up, "It's not—"

"Nah, Taeja. Don't explain shit," Strap interrupted. "I'm still tryna understand why you snuck out the house to go eat out with ya ex."

"I didn't *sneak* anywhere, Strap! That's what *you* did!"

"I'm sorry, but I'm going to have to ask you all to leave," the hostess interrupted, kneeling down in front of Strap to pick up the restaurant buzzer. "You're creating a disturbance."

Strap stared at Fallon furiously. "C'mon, Tae." Following his lead, Taeja exited behind him.

Fallon turned to get Cash, but he'd already left. *When did he leave?* She marched out the door, trailing a few feet behind Strap and Taeja. *And he's still carrying that damn baby!* "Damien! Damien!!!"

"I'll talk to you later, Fallon," Strap asserted. "I don't know what the fuck I might say right now." He meant it. A flurry of different emotions washed over him, from regret, betrayal, hurt, and even hate. Strap was livid!

Damn. I think I know exactly how Cash felt! he thought. *Does Fallon think she can have both of us?!* He felt stupid for wanting to build a future with her. *Maybe Ghost was right— fuck her! Give a female loyalty and she don't know how to act.*

Neither one of them had taken into consideration how their own situations looked on the outside. Instead, both were fuming.

"No! You're gonna talk to me now!" Fallon sprinted after them, tugging on Strap's arm forcefully.

"Don't put your hands on me, Fallon!" He set the baby's car seat on the ground next to him. Strap raised his hands, pulling away from her. "Get the hell on, now!"

"No! Who the fuck is this bitch to you?! And whose baby is this?!"

"Taeja," Strap called, ignoring Fallon's questions. Taking his keys from his pocket, he tossed them to her. "Go take the baby and get in the car, please. I'll take y'all to eat somewhere else." Taeja nodded and followed his directions.

"Damien, have you lost your mind?!" Fallon hissed. "Y'all rode together too?! I can't believe you."

"She's just a friend! There ain't shit goin' on between me and her!"

"Niggas are never just friends with females!" Fallon rolled her eyes. "You must think I'm stupid!"

"Nah, Fallon. You must think *I* am. You hugged up and shit on my brother at a restaurant after *lying* to me about who you was goin' with! That's fucked up!"

"It wasn't like that!" she protested. "He told me—"

"I don't give a fuck, Fallon. You probably just gon' lie any damn way."

"Wow, really, Damien? You think I'm a liar?" Her voice revealed the hurt she felt.

"I don't think. I *know*," he corrected.

"You can ask Cash!" Fallon called after Strap's retreating figure.

"I'm good."

Fallon sighed. *I can't believe this just happened...* She trudged towards her car somberly. *He's calling me a liar? No way. He asks me out to eat but then takes another chick out? These men nowadays are a mess!*

Cash was propped up against her BMW, talking on his cell phone. "Yeah. Okay…" He looked at Fallon suspiciously then returned his attention to the caller. "Yeah."

"Why did you leave?" Fallon asked the moment he put his phone away.

"Why would I stay?" Cash shrugged. "That shit had nothin' to do with me."

"You could've told him it wasn't what it looked like!"

"Why *didn't* you tell him you were gonna meet up with me?" he asked curiously.

Fallon shrugged. "I didn't think it was a big deal," she lied.

Cash snickered. He'd half expected that answer from her. "I'm startin' to think you might be a compulsive liar, Fallon."

"I'm not," she said weakly. She wasn't in the mood to argue with him. "If you think so then please get off my car so I can go home."

"I'll let you go in a second. I wanted to ask you about somethin'."

Fallon eyed him wearily. "What is it?"

"Why is Remy sayin' you're not pregnant?"

"W-what?" she stuttered. *Was it her that he was talking to just now? It had to be. He wasn't acting like this earlier.*

Cash got off the car and went to stand directly in front of her. "Prove to me you're not a liar. Is it true or not?"

"C um for me, Blaze!" Shantreis moaned silkily. Blaze looked her in the eyes before releasing himself inside of her. "Damn that was good," he mumbled, collapsing on top of her.

"I know," she joked, wrapping her arms around his sweaty body. It was nearing three o' clock in the afternoon and they'd spent their whole day in bed.

Blaze kissed her small belly, rubbing it gently. "I can't believe I'm about to be a daddy." He smiled. "My first son."

"It's a *seventy* percent chance," Shantreis reminded.

Her seventeen week checkup was yesterday and during the ultrasound, the tech said she thought it was a boy. It didn't really matter to Shantreis if it was a girl or boy. It may have sounded cliché but she just wanted their child to be healthy. Despite the doctor trying to ease her fears, she wasn't convinced that the abuse she'd taken from Outlaw hadn't caused some type of mental retardation.

"It's a boy. Trust me. I know."

"Get up," she said, hitting his back teasingly. "You said you were gonna take me to Saks today. I wanna show you some of the stuff I picked out at Babies 'R Us too."

"Treis, don't go in there thinkin' we gonna buy out the whole damn store," Blaze chided.

"Why not? We got it." She shrugged him off. "The garage sale is in a few days. I know I'm gonna make a lot off the shit in that house."

"That don't mean you need to spend it all, Treis."

Shantreis wrinkled her nose at him. Blaze was so damn practical. *Frugal ass,* she thought. He was still working at UPS even though he didn't need to. She both respected and resented it at the same time.

She couldn't explain how close they had become in such a short period of time. It was something that just happened. They'd always had undeniable chemistry but she underestimated it when they fell out back when Outlaw was alive.

If I had just chose Blaze after he stole the money, how much different would life be? she wondered. *Probably the same. Only difference is that Outlaw wouldn't be dead.*

For whatever reason, his death still fucked with her. The nightmares hadn't completely stopped, but Shantreis was doing better than before. She prayed every night in hopes that would help.

"Ay, c'mon," Blaze called out to her, snapping her back to reality. "Take a shower with me."

In about two hours, they finally made it out the house and to the mall. As promised, Shantreis was on a strict budget. He'd only let her spend three thousand dollars, but considering everything was for the baby, she ended up with a good amount of things.

"What you wanna eat?" Blaze asked as they took a seat at the food court.

"I'm not really hungry," she admitted. "But I got a cravin' for a Cinnabon." She smiled playfully.

Blaze shook his head. "All you ever eat is junk, baby. You gotta start eatin' better."

Blah blah, she thought. He would lecture her, but he always gave in to her requests. "Thank you, bae," she called after him.

Shantreis dug into one of the bags, pulling out a small pair of Burberry baby booties. *What will our child look like, I wonder...*

She smiled, imagining a little miniature Blaze. *Awww...* Then, just as quickly as the thought had come, her imagination created a baby resembling Outlaw.

Shantreis frowned, tossing the booties back into the bag. *Hell no.* The truth of the matter was she didn't know who the father was. Blaze was confident, but she wasn't.

Screech!

What the hell? Shantreis looked up. A girl pulled out a chair at their table and took a seat. She held a cup of Starbucks coffee in her hand and she was tall as hell. *Damn Amazon bitch. Why the fuck is she here?* Her brown skintone and shoulder-length hair put Shantreis in the mind of Keshia Knight Pulliam from The House of Payne.

Do I know this bitch? For a few moments, they just stared at one another. *What are we having—a staring contest or some shit? This bitch bold as hell too. Just because I'm pregnant doesn't mean I won't check a bitch.*

"Can I help you?" Shantreis asked mockingly. "Do I know you or you just retarded or some shit?"

The girl smiled smugly at her. "I think *I* know you... You're Outlaw's girlfriend, right?"

"Who are you?" Shantreis's eyes narrowed, refusing to confirm or deny the question. "Were you one of his jump-offs?"

She laughed. "I never fucked with him a day in my life."

Shantreis didn't believe it, but she wasn't about to press the issue. At the end of the day, she didn't give a damn. "Why the fuck are—"

"London, what the hell are you doin'?" Blaze piped up.

Shantreis stared at him in confusion. *So he knows this bitch?* She examined him closer. Was Blaze *nervous?*

"You're not going to introduce us, Jacob?" the woman asked calmly. She was talking to Blaze, but her eyes remained fixed on Shantreis.

This bitch knows his government?

"London, this is my baby momma Shantreis. Shantreis—"

"Your baby momma?" Shantreis stood up from her chair so quickly it toppled over. "That's my title now? Who is this bitch then?"

She didn't know if his initial statement hurt more or the next one that came thoughtlessly flying from his lips. "What do you mean? You *are* my baby momma. What do you want me to say?"

"Nigga, don't try to flex on me over this bitch!" Shantreis shouted. Her hormones had her feeling sensitive as hell.

Blaze looked genuinely confused. "Do we need to talk? C'mon. Let's go talk somewhere private." He reached for Shantreis's arm but she yanked it away.

"Who the fuck are you supposed to be?!" Shantreis asked, meeting the girl's intense gaze. "Bitch, if you supposed to be his girlfriend then you stupider than you look! I been over this nigga's house for the past few weeks! Where the hell have you been?"

"Shantreis," Blaze started, attempting to calm her down.

"If he's not claiming you then obviously—" London started.

"Shut the fuck up, London!" Blaze interrupted.

"I'm fuckin' good! You can have this bitch, nigga!" Shantreis picked up her bags. "Gimme the fuckin' keys, Blaze!" They rode together but they sure as hell weren't leaving together.

"Treis, that's *my* fuckin' car! You think I'm a' let you leave me stranded?!" he growled.

"It's cuz of me you got that fuckin' car! That shit is basically mine!" She looked over at London. "I'm sure she'll take you home unless the bum bitch ain't got a car."

"Just hear me out cuz you sound stupid as fuck right now!" he tried to explain.

"Nah. Don't explain shit to me. I'm just your *baby momma*," Shantreis said sarcastically. "Gimme the keys."

"Stop it, Treis!" Blaze yelled when she came towards him, reaching for his pockets.

"Gimme the fuckin' keys then!!!" she nearly screamed. If they didn't already have the attention of everyone sitting in the Triangle Town Center food court, they did now.

Shantreis kept lunging violently to get access to the keys, but he pushed her back gently each time. "Stop 'fore you get hurt, now!" Blaze grabbed her wrists, keeping her at a distance of arm's length.

"Nigga, you gonna put your hands on a bitch that's pregnant?!"

"I didn't say that, Treis! Don't twist my words!"

"Fuck it!" she yelled, finally giving up. "Let go of me! I'll get my own damn ride home!" Shantreis picked up her bags and looked at London furiously.

Whap!

Shantreis popped her in the mouth roughly. "Bitch!"

"Oh hell no!" London screamed, but Blaze restrained her before she could reach Shantreis.

Despite the scene that just transpired, Shantreis glided out gracefully. She slid her D&G shades onto her eyes so no one could see the tears finally falling down her face.

"What did you say?" Ghost asked, not believing that he'd heard correctly.

"These niggas just came up to my job askin' about you," Malaysia informed him. "I told them I ain't know shit. But, bae—"

"I'm a' call you back." Ghost didn't give her a chance to reply. He disconnected the call. *Fuck*. He slouched back on the sofa. *Time to settle this shit...*

Ghost dialed a number he hadn't used in a long time. He sighed as the phone started ringing. On the third ring, Cash finally answered.

"Who this?"

"Whassup, brother?" Ghost greeted scornfully.

"Ghost. Thought I would a' heard from you sooner. I got your message about you bein' back in town," Cash sneered.

"Shit, nigga, you know me. No muh'fucka could *ever* push me out my city."

"You should a' stayed where you was. Fuckin' around with me you'll be in the dirt soon..."

"Yeah. Like Outlaw, right?" Ghost knew that would get under his skin. Just that quickly he'd forgotten the whole point of calling.

"You talk a lot of shit for a nigga that ain't came to see me yet. I *know* you wouldn't run up on my ass the way you did Quon."

"Nigga, you fuckin' crazy if you believe that shit."

"Then why didn't you?" Cash snickered. "Nigga, I ain't hard to find."

Ghost's jaw tightened. He hated for a nigga to try and call him out. "Yeah. You right. I seen you and ya girl over Grandma Chick's but I spared ya ass. Now I'm startin' to regret that shit."

If Ghost saw me at Grandma Chick's and could a' got a shot in, then it's time to start handing out pink slips, Cash thought.

Cash kept a team of shooters watching his back anytime he went out, but he never completely put his guard down. They were just an added security in place for overly ambitious niggas like Ghost. Many wanted the notoriety of saying they killed a legend like Cash, but few had the balls to deal with the consequences if they missed. That fact alone kept most from trying him.

Ghost grinned at Cash's silence. He knew that would shut him up. Truthfully he didn't see them. The only reason he knew was because Taeja sent Malaysia a text message relaying what happened earlier. Malaysia was always telling him her friends' business. *Like I care about that bullshit.* Today was the only exception.

"That's not why I called you though," Ghost continued. "I wanted to dead this beef shit."

"Nigga, what?" Cash asked incredulously. "You get on the phone poppin' ya dick sucker about—"

"I know who killed Outlaw," he butted in. "I heard you been askin' the streets but nobody sayin' shit."

Cash sucked his teeth. "You expect me to believe you would know? Nigga, I wouldn't be surprised if you did the shit! Go 'head though. Tell me. I'll humor you."

"Take the bounty off my head and I will."

"Done."

Cash consented easier than Ghost thought he would. What he failed to realize was at the end of the day, Cash had nothing to lose. If Ghost was bullshitting him, he'd kill him. Up until this point, he hadn't really put in a conscious effort to find his brother. The bounty was still there, but Cash left it up to those niggas to cash in. With all the bullshit that recently resurfaced in his life, he had more important matters to worry about.

"Let me warn you now," Cash inserted. *"Don't* play wit' me, Ghost. You tell me some bullshit and I'll murk ya ass personally."

"Yeah whatever." Ghost snorted. "It was his bitch… Shantreis."

Chapter 14

"Your call has been forwarded to an automated voice messaging system. 919…"

Fallon disconnected the call with a pout. She had been blowing up Strap's phone. From sending him texts to leaving voicemails, she'd done it all. All of her messages were filled with curses and threats. If she'd had Taeja's number, she would—

I do! Her mind went back to their run in at Target. Taeja had given her a scrap of paper with her phone number. *Where did I put it?* Fallon rifled through her purse looking for it. *If I could've followed them then I wouldn't have to do all this. If only Cash hadn't slowed me down.*

Cash… Her mind reflected on their last conversation.

"Prove to me you're not a liar. Is it true or not?" Cash *demanded, looking at her expectantly.*

Did she send him the recording? Fallon wondered. If Remy did and then Fallon denied it, she would be indisputably proving his point.

Still, her common sense flew out the window when she opened her mouth.

"*I have no reason to lie to you, Damontrez. If you're starting to have second thoughts then—*"

Cash held us his hand. "Fine. I'll take your word for it. When's your doctor appointment? I'll come with you."

Fallon narrowed her eyes. "Because you think I'm lying?"

"*No. I should be there, shouldn't I? When is it?" he repeated.*

"*I let my appointment card at home. I'll text it to you then."*

Cash nodded. "A'ight. But listen, Fallon, if you really did some lowdown shit like that—"

"*You don't have to worry about that," she lied.*

Fallon sighed. It was at that moment that Cash texted her.

Still aint heard nthn from u. Txt me the info.

Fallon tossed her phone across the room in annoyance. She had stopped taking her medication and her "morning sickness" had subsided. Still, her period hadn't come on so that gave her the tiniest glimmer of hope. *If I'm not pregnant, that doesn't necessarily mean I lied. I'll just tell him the test gave me a false reading. That kind of thing happens all the time, right?*

Thinking about it made her head hurt. Fallon hopped up, heading to her laundry hamper. It was possible she'd stuffed the slip of paper with Taeja's number in her pocket. She tossed her clothes out wildly until she spotted a pair of boyfriend jeans. *Those.* Fallon went through the pockets frantically. *Yes! Got it!*

She waited impatiently as the phone rang. She didn't know exactly what she was going to say, but she was definitely going to cuss that bitch out.

"Fallon, don't do this."

"Strap?" she asked, not believing it was his voice on the other end of the receiver. "Oh. You can pick up this bitch's phone but you can't pick up when I call yours?!"

"My phone is dead."

"Boy, please. I don't believe that! Where the hell are you at? I see you're still with Taeja!"

Strap sighed dejectedly. She was still turned up but his voice sounded drained... fed up. "I have to take her home, Fallon. Don't call her phone no more, a'ight? Your problem is with me. I'll call you when I get home."

Click.

"So you're not coming here?" Fallon yelled to the air. *I can't believe him.* She contemplated calling back anyway but decided against it. She tossed her phone on the bed and walked into the bathroom. As Fallon sat down relieving her bladder, she thought about everything going on with her life.

My life is fucked up. I lost my fiancé because I slept with his brother. Now his brother is cheating on me with my old friend. I can't stop lying to save my life. Is this karma paying me back?

Fallon wiped herself but what she saw in the tissue alarmed her. *Blood?* Her heart sank. *My period's coming on?* She closed her eyes, disappointed. *I guess that answers the question. I'm* not *pregnant.*

"Thanks for bringing Kairi up," Taeja said. They were back at her apartment. Strap offered to carry the heavy carseat upstairs and uncharacteristically, she accepted his offer. She'd put Kairi in her crib already. She and Strap now stood in front of the door.

"I appreciate you taking us out to eat, too." He'd treated them to The Pit, a barbeque restaurant on West Davie. "You really didn't have to."

"No problem. I wanted to." His troubled face finally gave her a smile.

Although Strap had been trying to pretend he wasn't bothered by the day's prior events, Taeja could tell it was still weighing heavily on his mind. They hadn't spoken about it and Taeja left it alone. She didn't want to pry. It wasn't any of her business anyway. No words were exchanged even after Fallon called her phone. Strap just apologized for it.

"Well, you drive home safe..." her voice trailed off awkwardly.

"Look, Taeja," Strap sighed. "I'm real sorry about what happened."

"It's okay. It's not your fault."

"Nah. It *is* my fault. I put you in a very uncomfortable situation earlier. That was never my intention," he told her sincerely, looking directly into her eyes.

"Well, I hope y'all can work it out," she said half-heartedly. Taeja cleared her throat trying to clear away her true feelings. *How insensitive would I be to discuss him and me?* Besides, she could look straight in his eyes and tell how much he adored Fallon. Secretly she wished she had a man that looked at her like that... not just any man... but him... Strap...

"I don't know, man." Strap shook his head. He leaned against the door and looked at the ceiling. "It's so much bullshit."

"You wanna be with her though, right?"

Strap was quiet. He didn't know how to answer that.

"You'll feel better after you figure it out. Maybe you two need to take a time out," she suggested truthfully.

He shrugged in response. "I feel like I give her everything and don't get shit back in return. All I want is loyalty, Tae. That ain't too much to ask is it?"

"No. Not at all." Taeja shook her head in understanding. "That's all I want, too. Whenever I get a man… I'll put him first and he'll do the same for me." Her voice was wistful.

"Yeah." Strap nodded. "That's *exactly* how it's supposed to be. You'll make some nigga out here lucky one day."

"I want to make you happy," she mumbled under her breath.

"Huh?"

Without thinking, she pressed her body to him and kissed his lips softly. For a moment, Strap stood still and Taeja began to regret her actions. She started to pull back, but was pleasantly surprised when he deepened the kiss. She parted her lips, allowing his tongue access.

Strap's hands glided up her hips, roaming her upper body passionately. Taeja walked them towards the sofa, never breaking their embrace. Her breaths were shallow. A small moan fell from her lips as he pressed his body closer to hers.

"Oooh, Damien…" Taeja pulled away from him for a moment to slip her shirt off. After tossing it away, revealing her pink lace bra, she laid back on the sofa. Strap hovered over her, alternating between fervently kissing her mouth and neck.

Taeja's fingertips brushed against the fly of his jeans, anticipating what was concealed behind the thick fabric. She could feel his hardness and wondered what it would feel like to have him inside of her.

"Baby, please—" she started, but the sudden sound of Kairi crying cut her off.

As if Strap had been hypnotized, Kairi's hollering snapped him out of it. He was painfully aware of what just happened. "I should probably go."

"No! Wait! I'll be right back!" Taeja said, making her way down the hallway. "It'll be real quick."

Strap sighed and slouched against the sofa. *Damn. I fucked up.* He was glad they hadn't taken it any further but it escalated quickly nonetheless. When Taeja came back, he was going to apologize and leave. He didn't want her to feel bad but they shouldn't have crossed the line. *Not when I'm technically still with Fallon… It ain't fair to either one of them.*

He surveyed her coffee table and helped himself to the candy dish sitting on top of it. Several small 5x7 pictures decorated the table. There was a picture of a baby that was obviously Kairi when she was born. The rest were pictures of people Strap assumed were her family—grandparents and her father. However, there was one picture in particular that stood out to him.

A teenage version of Taeja sat next to another girl. They favored each other slightly, sharing the same doe-shaped eyes and pouty, heart-shaped lips. *That's got to be her sister,* he thought. *But why does she look so familiar?*

"That's my sister Vanessa." Taeja reappeared, taking a seat next to him. "Kairi's mom."

Taeja rested her head on his shoulder. "We weren't really close since I lived with our dad in Smithfield. She stayed here with our Grandma." She sighed. "She was always getting into some bullshit running behind Keef, her sorry ass baby's father. He was into that street shit real hard." Tears distorted her voice as she recounted what happened.

"'Nessa left one night saying she was going to the club. My Grandma didn't hear from her the next day, but didn't think anything of it at first. 'Nessa was always doing that—leaving for days—but she always called to check up on Kairi..." Taeja said, choking up on her tears.

Strap gripped her tighter. "It's okay, Taeja. You don't have to talk about it if it's painful."

"No. I'm okay..." she insisted, composing herself enough to continue, "We tried to get in contact with her friend Rinashia because they went together, but her family didn't hear from her either. They both went missing that night."

"Rinashia? Her nickname was Ri-Ri?" Strap asked as the screws in his brain started to turn.

Taeja nodded.

He nearly choked on his peppermint as the realization swept over him. *Damn! That's her!*

"Did you know her?" she sniffed.

"Yeah..." His face almost betrayed his thoughts but he played it off. "My brother used to talk to her before he started dating Malaysia."

I can't believe this shit, he thought. *Vanessa is Taeja's sister! The chick that tried to set me and Ghost up so her baby daddy could rob us.*

Strap remembered that night vividly. The way Ghost had beat Vanessa's ass when he found out... he'd beat her so brutally that he'd knocked her unconscious. The way Strap knocked Ri-Ri out with the butt of his gun... how callously he put both girls in the trunk. The way they'd met

Woo on New Bern so he could dispose of their bodies… Strap didn't know how Woo had ultimately killed them but he assumed it was probably painful. Like some shit out of a horror movie. The fact that every single body they'd given him to dispose of had never been recovered made him come to that conclusion.

"You didn't hear about it?" Taeja asked. "It was on the news a few weeks ago but nobody knows anything! I just can't believe that! A club full of people and nobody saw who my sister left with?! That's bullshit!

"Her baby's father was found murdered the day after. I think whoever killed him may have killed her too. He was a wannabe thug so I think he got 'Nessa caught up in some street shit." Her voice was full of scorn. "I just don't understand it! The police couldn't find her body so we couldn't even give her a proper funeral!" Taeja sobbed, finally breaking down. She buried her head in Strap's chest, clinging to him tightly like a lost child.

"I'm sorry, baby. I'm so sorry," Strap said sincerely, feeling guilt settling on his shoulders.

Damn… he thought. *I should a' just told Ghost to let the shit go. We could a' just dealt with them niggas instead.* Hell, he knew Ghost had been the one to kill Keef. He'd bragged to Strap about it the very next day.

Strap had never regretted taking anyone's life until now. Most times he felt his victims' deaths were well-deserved. None of those niggas were innocent. They had always done something to warrant losing their lives. Ten times out of ten they understood the possible repercussions, but they were foolhardy enough to try it anyway. Whether it was for street fame, money, or respect, there would always be a price to pay to get it. That was how the game went.

Still... They was females... We didn't have to kill them. Granted, Strap hadn't been the one to actually kill either one, but he'd played a part in it. If ever there was a time he wished for the ability to take things back, it was now. Knowing what he'd inadvertently done to her family fucked him up inside.

Chapter 15

Shantreis was beyond pissed! As if the shit with Blaze and London wasn't enough, Fallon wasn't answering the damn phone either! All of her other associates were tied to Outlaw and she didn't want them to know where she was currently laying her head. *I can't believe I had to ride the damn Amigo Taxi back to the condo. That shit cost me thirty fuckin' dollars.*

She heard the keys jiggling in the lock and cursed silently to herself. *I wanted to be gone before this nigga got back.* She probably would've been closer to finishing if she hadn't taken the liberty of bleaching some of Blaze's shit.

"Shantreis!" Blaze shouted. "Shantreis!"

She was silent as she alternated between putting her things in big, black trash bags and her Louis Vuitton suitcases. *I knew I should've left some of my shit at the old house.* Shantreis had countless articles of clothing to pack, along with the baby's things. On top of that, she was going to have to take several trips back and forth to the parking garage.

This dumb ass nigga, she thought. *I can't believe he had a girlfriend!*

"I'm just his baby momma," Shantreis scoffed at his introduction of her. "You know what I went through with Outlaw and you would do this dumb shit?!" *He got another fuckin' bitch... Niggas ain't shit! I knew he was just like every other nigga!*

"What the fuck are you doin'?" Blaze stood in the doorway. "Why are you packin' ya shit?"

Shantreis rolled her eyes. "So you can move your bitch London in. Fuck you, nigga!"

He sighed. "Baby, c'mere and talk to me." Blaze tried to grab her wrist but she snatched away from him.

"Nigga, don't 'baby' me! I'm just your baby momma, Blaze?!" As she spoke tears lined her eyes. Shantreis hated the way her hormones were affecting her. Right now she just wanted to cry and scream. "Just your fuckin' baby momma?!!!"

"That's why you mad?" he asked simply. "Because of how I introduced you?! Should I have said you was my ol' lady?"

Shantreis was silent. She had too much pride to admit that was what she wanted. The amused smirk on his face pissed her off even more. *Does he think this shit is a game?*

"You tell me what the fuck we were doin' then! Playin' house or some shit?! Bitch, you got me fucked up! I don't need this shit. I don't need a damn man either."

"Treis, chill the fuck out."

That damn smirk was still on his face.

"I didn't want yo' ass anyway! You ain't got enough money."

That was the one way to get under Blaze's skin. Seeing his bemused expression fade, Shantreis felt better.

"You still on that greedy, gold digging shit, huh?" he asked seriously.

"Fuck you, Blaze! I got my own!"

"Only cuz you killed that muthafucka! If not, yo' ass would be sittin' in somebody's projects right now lookin' for a nigga to buy you!"

"To buy me?!" Shantreis narrowed her eyebrows. "Nigga, please!" She returned her attention to packing her things. "Fuck you! When I walk out today, you ain't gotta worry about seein' me no more!"

"What the fuck does that mean? You tryna say you ain't gonna let me see my baby either, Treis?!"

"It probably ain't even your baby anyway!"

"What?!" Blaze yelled. His tone suggested her statement was impossible. "Man, fuck that! I know it's mine."

Shantreis rolled her eyes. "Please! I know you don't think me and a nigga I was *living with* was using condoms!"

"Let you tell it, you weren't fuckin' that nigga no more!"

"Me and you always used condoms," Shantreis persisted. "I can count on my fingers how many times we didn't and you *always* pulled out!"

"You sure about that?"

"Yeah!" She looked at him in disbelief. "What are you sayin'?"

Blaze shrugs. "Condoms ain't a hundred percent effective. Shit happens."

Shantreis screwed up her face. "Shit happens? Fuck you mean? Shit ain't happen unless *you made* it happen!!! A bitch was far from pressed to have a baby by your broke…" Her voice trailed off, taking his statement a different way. *I wouldn't be pressed, but Blaze would…*

"Wait a minute. Did you…. Did you do it? You fucked up the condoms? You trapped me?!"

"But you said it probably ain't my kid though," he said nonchalantly.

"Nah. Answer the question directly! You did that shit?!"

Blaze shrugged in response.

Shantreis dropped to the floor in shock. To her, he was confirming her suspicions. If he hadn't then he would've just came out and said no. *Now this nigga too ashamed to admit it!* Her life was perfect until he'd stepped in and played God. *Outlaw had changed! He was treating me right! We didn't have to worry about Kaleesha anymore! We were happy! I had even gotten over Blaze! I can't believe he would do all this to keep me in his life!*

Shantreis had heard the stories many times before—of niggas trapping females—but she'd never imagined she would become a victim. She thought Blaze had more sense than that. Obviously she was wrong.

"I-I can't believe you! Blaze, you ruined my fuckin' life!" She lunged at him, pounding him with her fists.

He allowed her to get a few hits in before restraining her. "Baby, calm down…"

"Let go of me!" Shantreis squealed, wriggling around in his arms until he released her. "You fucked up my life! I hate yo' ass!" She walked out of the room. She didn't even give a fuck about her clothes anymore.

"Baby, can we talk about this shit? It don't matter how it happened! We together now!" Blaze tried to justify himself as he followed her out into the foyer.

"Nigga, did you forget about London?! She can have yo' ass! I don't want you no more."

Blaze sucked his teeth. "London's my cousin! She's Filthy's sister! She just wanted to know why I ain't show up to the funeral and where Filthy is!"

"You expect me to believe that?"

"Why would I lie to you?! You said it yourself! I'm *always* spendin' my fuckin' time with you! I ain't got time for no other bitch!" He tried to look into her eyes but she refused to face him. "You bein' all jealous and shit was a turn on, especially since you used to act like you ain't give a fuck about me."

Shantreis shook her head, stopping at the front door. Whether or not she believed him was irrelevant now. The truth about their baby couldn't be denied. *He dead wrong for this! This nigga basically controlled my life! Everything he wanted, he got. That shit ain't right. He gotta pay the consequences.*

"I'm not keepin' this baby, Blaze."

"What did you say?"

Her voice was void of any emotions as she clarified it for him. "I'm getting an abortion."

Why hasn't Strap called me? Fallon thought as she turned into her apartment complex. Never in a million years did she imagine she would be this pressed over Strap and his whereabouts. He had always chased after her so this was new for her. *This is so unlike him. He wouldn't just not call me.*

It was ironic. She'd brushed off his feelings for her and rejected him many times before. Fallon had even convinced herself she didn't love him as anything more than a brother for the longest time. Now the thought of potentially losing him was affecting her harder than she'd expected.

Did he get hurt or something? Get in trouble? Fallon had easily forgotten about the types of things Strap did to earn a living. He claimed he was turning over a new leaf but who could say for sure? Old habits die hard. *What if someone tried to get revenge on him?*

Frantically she pulled out her phone. "Call Ghost," she instructed her phone. *He'll know something.*

"I don't see 'Go' in your address book," Siri informed. "Would you like me to—?"

"Ghost!" Fallon shouted, but as she reached her building she immediately cancelled the call.

Strap was outside, sitting on the trunk of his car. Her eyes immediately lit up. Fallon whipped into the parking space next to him. She hopped out quickly, completely forgetting the groceries sitting in her passenger seat.

"Damien! Where the hell have you been?!" Fallon shouted, observing his body for any signs of injury.

"At the crib," he replied nonchalantly.

She frowned. "I was worried."

"Oh yeah?" Strap seemed slightly surprised but his voice and facial expression remained solemn. "But look, I came through cuz we need to talk about some shit… What's really up with you and my brother? Y'all tryna get back together?"

Fallon looked at him quizzically, raising an eyebrow. "What? Are you kidding me, Damien?! I know you're not talking! You're going out looking like a family with some random bi—"

Strap raised his hand to silence her, quickly losing his calm demeanor. "Fuck what you think cuz you don't know shit!" He jumped off the back of the car and stood directly in front of her. "Answer the question! Why would you go out to eat with him but then tell me you're goin' out with Shantreis? Why was you all hugged up on that nigga?!"

"Nah. I thought you said I was a liar and I was just going to lie about it, anyway?" Fallon asked mockingly, bringing up his stinging words from the restaurant that day. She feigned hurt, but she was only stalling. She was trying desperately to come up with an excuse but nothing came to mind. Fallon really didn't know why she didn't tell Strap. Maybe his accusations weren't completely unfounded. "Quit yelling at me like I'm your child!"

Strap looked at her, still awaiting her response. He wasn't about to play into Fallon's childish antics. All he wanted was answers. "C'mon, Fallon, you got defensive and shit when I called you out about wearin' his ring that time, too. Stop with the bullshit."

Fallon blew her breath before throwing her hands up in the air. "Fine. I don't know, okay?! I just did!" she admitted.

He nodded his head. "A'ight." He walked along the side of his car, preparing to get inside but Fallon grabbed him by the arm.

"Where are you going?!"

Strap removed her hand before answering, "Goin' back home."

"Why? You didn't even explain yourself yet! How did you know Taeja? Why were y'all out on a date?"

He chuckled and shook his head condescendingly. "It wasn't a date."

"Like hell if it didn't look like one!" she hollered. She looked at him impatiently. "I'm waiting. Tell me."

"For what, Fallon? It don't even matter anymore."

"Why doesn't it?" Fallon's confusion showed as she scrunched up her face. "Are you breaking up with me?"

"Were we ever truly in a relationship, Fallon? Be real, now. Cash still got yo' fuckin' heart and I can't do that sharin' shit. We rushed into this shit. That was a big fuckin' mistake... I can't do this shit with you no more, Fallon. You don't know what the hell you want. I should've walked away the first time but Taeja convinced me not to."

"Are you serious? *She*, of all people, is the reason you came back to my house that day?" *How long has he known this bitch? Taeja's up here giving him advice on how to handle our relationship problems?*

"She told me if I loved you, I should forgive you and concentrate on our future." Strap nodded thoughtfully. "I love you, but I ain't gettin' shit back in return. At least not the way it's supposed to be. I *know* you don't love me half as much as I love you, Fallon. I'm just a fuckin' backup—a consolation price cuz you can't have Cash!"

Fallon looked hurt, but Strap knew she wasn't anywhere close to feeling the pain he did at that moment. He'd wanted so badly to have her, to be the man she wanted and needed but how could he when she always had one eye still focused on his brother?

"And to tell you the truth," Strap continued. "You was right when you said I shouldn't risk the relationship I got with my brother. I was mad because I wanted your loyalty but you couldn't even give that to Cash! And I know that nigga gave you everything! What the fuck was I thinkin'?!"

"Fuck you, Strap!" Fallon shouted as her eyes started to well up with tears. It was the only thing she could think to say. Deep down inside, she knew he was right. They *had* rushed into it. She barely had enough time to get over Cash. *It's only been about a month.*

Fallon definitely had feelings for Strap, regardless of what he may have thought. Would she call it love? Maybe not, but she reasoned it was close enough. Their timing was just off. Still, something seemed different to her. *It's always been this way but it's never been a problem before. Why the sudden change?* she wondered.

"That's not really it, is it? It's because of Taeja! It's gotta be!" She nodded with conviction. "You liked me for five years straight, Strap! Now all of a sudden you're giving up on me? That doesn't make any sense. You practically worship the ground I walk on! You probably love me more than you love yourself!"

Wow. Strap noted Fallon's arrogance and frowned. He'd always felt like she took him for granted, but this was confirmation. The realization gave him reassurance that he was doing the right thing. "You think you can do whatever the fuck you want and I'm always gonna be here? A nigga fed up, Fallon."

"I don't believe you," she murmured, shaking her head. "There's got to be another reason."

He sighed. "This doesn't have shit to do with that girl. It's about me and *you.* We keep doin' the same shit! It's gettin' old! You know I'm right so why deny it?" Strap wiped away the lone tear that rolled down her cheek and softened his tone. "Think about it. Keep it 100 with yourself, sweetheart, cuz I already know. If you could have either one of us right now, who would you choose? Cash or me?"

Fallon sniffled as she considered his question. "I-I don't know."

He nodded. "I know," he said gently. "Goodbye, Fallon."

Chapter 16

"Kaleesha! Did you know that bitch having a yard sale?!"

"What are you talkin' about, Ashlyn?" Kaleesha pulled the phone away from her ear. "Who?"

"Shantreis!" she exclaimed. "I went up there and bought a Speedy 40 bag for $400! She's selling her Celine bag too for only—"

"I don't give a damn! Outlaw bought me that kinda shit too!" Kaleesha rolled her eyes. She refused to sell her bags even though she could use the money. Her status was important to her. She liked people thinking she was *that* bitch. A boss bitch.

"Anyway, I was just tryna tell you so you can go over there. She's selling the townhouse too! My point is that bitch is paid. You need to make her give you some money."

Kaleesha nodded. Cash had looked out for her a few days ago, so she could get her car out the shop and pay a few bills off. Still, she didn't want to continue to be dependent upon him. He'd already made it clear he was only doing it for Monet's sake. *That nigga stingy as hell. I know he got it but he only gave me three thousand dollars.*

"You still over there?" Kaleesha asked.

"Nah. I just left. It's not much stuff left. She got 'paid' tags on the furniture and shit. It's supposed to end soon. You already out?"

"Yeah. I am. Thanks, Ash." She disconnected the call and peered in the rearview mirror to look at her daughter. "You wanna get a Happy Meal, Mo-Mo?"

Monet nodded. If Kaleesha hadn't been looking at her, she wouldn't have even known she'd responded.

Kaleesha sighed despondently. Monet hadn't spoken since the day she picked her up with Tony. She was like a completely different child. Monet never talked or smiled anymore. She always seemed nervous. Kaleesha had done some research on the internet and found that sometimes children were mute after a traumatic incident.

She really loved her daddy, Kaleesha thought. Her heart hurt to see her child suffering this way. She made a mental note to set an appointment for Monet to see a doctor next week. *Surely they can do something.*

After making a quick run to McDonald's, Kaleesha made her way over to the old neighborhood. As she turned down the street, she could see cars lining the street and a mill of people in the yard.

I thought Ashlyn said she would be ending it soon? She glanced at the clock on the dash. *Oh well. Fuck it.* Boldly Kaleesha pulled into the driveway. Her eyes scanned the yard for Shantreis. *She must be inside.*

"Excuse me, ma'am," a man greeted her as she stepped out of the car. "You can't park here."

"Who are you?" Kaleesha crinkled her nose.

"I work here."

This bitch got workers? "I'll move after I see Shantreis." She opened the back door to let Monet out but she wouldn't budge.

Frantically Monet shook her head back and forth. A strange, small whimpering sound came from her mouth.

"Baby, what's wrong?" Kaleesha asked, puzzled by her daughter's reaction. "You don't wanna get out?"

Monet shook her head.

"I can't let you sit in the car, baby. C'mon." Kaleesha reached over her for the seatbelt but Monet put her small hands in the way to stop her.

"Kaleesha, what the hell are you doin' here?" Shantreis's voice came up behind her.

"For what you owe me." She held out her hand expectantly. "I believe some of the money you made today is mine."

Shantreis frowned. "Where would you get a stupid idea like that?"

"Some of the shit you're sellin' is Outlaw's. I'm the mother of his child and—"

"Bitch, you far off base with that logic. You ain't gettin' a penny. This is *my* hustle." Shantreis flashed a couple of big faces at Kaleesha patronizingly. "Maybe you should sell some of your old shit if you're that hard up."

"*Outlaw* would want his daughter to be taken care of."

"I don't give a fuck what Outlaw would've wanted. That nigga ain't here." Shantreis turned away. "Get the fuck off my lawn. This is private property, bitch."

"Shantreis, I will beat your ass!"

"You would hit a pregnant woman?"

"Pregnant?!" Shantreis's announcement caught Kaleesha off guard. "It's Outlaw's?"

"Yup." She smiled and looked at Monet. "Looks like you'll be gettin' a baby brother or baby sister."

Monet started howling. Her reaction caught Shantreis off guard. "What's wrong with her?"

Kaleesha was surprised too, but she wouldn't let on. Instead she thought of a wittier retort, "Who can blame her? I would hate to have a sibling by you too." Realizing she wouldn't get any money from Shantreis, she decided to leave before she embarrassed herself—or got hauled off to jail. Kaleesha wasn't sure which one.

Probably both, she thought.

"Monet, what was all that about?" Kaleesha asked as they headed back to Durham. She couldn't forget how nervous and jittery she was. *It's probably because we were at the house...*

"Sweetie, are you ever gonna talk to Mommy again? It makes me sad that you won't talk to me." Kaleesha's eyes watered up. The articles on the internet had advised against pressuring a child to speak after a traumatic event, but she couldn't help it.

Monet's expression now mirrored her own. Kaleesha immediately felt guilty for making her daughter feel bad. "I'm sorry, baby. It's just that Mommy can't help you if she doesn't know what's wrong with you." She sniffled, wiping her nose with the back of her wrist. "Is it because of Daddy? Daddy would want you to be happy and smiling. You don't want him looking down at you from Heaven being sad, do you?"

Then it happened... she spoke. Kaleesha had to strain her ears to pick up on her hushed tone.

"Daddy's not in Heaven because Daddy was a bad man."

"What?" Kaleesha shook her head, not believing the words she heard coming out of her daughter's mouth. She had her moments when she disliked Outlaw, but she'd *never* talked shit about him to Monet. "Who told you that?"

"If I don't want bad things to happen to me, I can't tell you."

"Here, you want some?" Taeja cooed at Kairi, waving a bag of Gerber Yogurt Melts around. It was Kairi's favorite snack. They had just bought them from Target.

"Here you go, booboo." She handed one to her niece with a smile, effectively calming her down. Kairi had cried hysterically when the cashier had to ring them up.

I can't wait to get a new car, Taeja thought as she opened the trunk to her 1997 Toyota Avalon. She'd had it since she turned old enough to drive. She looked enviously at the Jaguar XJL that pulled in next to her. *That's real nice… I'd like something like that.* Taeja chuckled bitterly. "How in the world would *I* be able to afford that?"

When she'd attended A&T majoring in Computer Science, Taeja thought she would be set for life. *I'm supposed to have a cushy job making 100,000 a year. I should be driving a new Mercedes E-class and living in a ritzy neighborhood.* Taeja sighed. She'd gotten a harsh dose of reality. *Now I'm in debt, making $10 an hour at Victoria's Secret.*

"Uhm. Mm." Kairi giggled and held out a treat for Taeja to eat.

"For me?" she asked, moving closer so Kairi could put it in her mouth. "Mmmm… Thank you, booboo."

"Mama, mama," Kairi babbled, offering her another.

"Say '*Tay juh*'," she sounded her name out but Kairi repeated 'Mama' over and over again anyway. Her eyes lowered, full of sadness. "I'm not your Mommy, sweetie."

Taeja sighed as she continued to put her groceries into the trunk. *At least I get to see Damien tonight.* Her mood immediately brightened. Malaysia had agreed to watch Kairi so she and Strap could go out. It had been a long time since she'd had the freedom or the money to truly go out and enjoy herself so Taeja couldn't wait!

"You like Damien too, huh, Kai?" The little girl giggled in response as Taeja bent over to buckle her into the carseat.

Since him and Fallon are broken up, it's even better, she thought. She'd been unable to contain her excitement when Strap told her.

"Excuse me, Miss Lady, how you doin'?"

Taeja was so startled she nearly bumped her head. Quickly she stood up, smiling uneasily at the man standing only inches away from her face. *Damn he's really close.*

"I'm good. Thank you," she said curtly.

"I'm Jimmy," he offered his hand for shake.

"Taeja." She didn't return the gesture. *I know I probably look rude as hell, but oh well. He needs to take a hint.*

Jimmy was overweight—at least a size 44—but had the audacity to squeeze his big ass in a pair of size 36 skinny jeans. The fitted, plaid button down shirt he donned didn't do him any favors either. *He looks like a damn fool.* Looking at him made her appreciate Strap's style even more. *I haven't seen a nigga that had shit on Damien.*

Jimmy squinted his eyes as he tried to peer at Kairi. Following his gaze, Taeja closed the door to obstruct his view.

"Ay, ain't that Keef's little girl?" he asked.

"Yes… Why?" Taeja placed her hand inside her purse discreetly, reaching for her mace. Ever since the day she'd almost gotten raped, she kept one on her person at all times. *In case this nigga tries anything stupid I'm prepared.*

He smiled widely. "That's what's up! Keef was my boy! I remember when her momma," he nudged his head in the direction of Kairi, "used to bring her over to the crib. She's still pretty as hell."

"Thank you."

"You one of Keef's peoples or…?"

Damn he nosy. "She's my sister's daughter."

"Oh…" Jimmy nodded knowingly. "Vanessa, right? My condolences, Taeja. It was real fucked up what happened to Keef and ol' girl. We wanted to get them niggas back but they damn near untouchable."

Taeja's ears perked up at his words. A million thoughts came rushing to her mind at once. "What did you say? What do you mean? Do you know something? Why didn't you tell the police? We need to tell the police if you know who did it."

"Nah." He shook his head. "Can't. It was them damn Hardy Boys."

"Who are they?"

Jimmy looked at her in surprise. "Damn. I thought everybody knew them. Them niggas Cash, Strap, and Ghost. We ain't got no concrete proof but I just *know* they had some shit to do with it. We was supposed to hit a lick that night but Vanessa called Keef back and told him not to come. Said she was comin' home but never did."

Taeja's mind was still focused on those names. "You said Strap? Is his real name Damien?"

"I don't know that nigga's government." Jimmy shrugged. "He got a close cut, bout 6'2, and dress like a pretty boy. Young nigga."

Oh my God! It can't be. She didn't want to believe it but the similarities were adding up. That was *definitely* his description. Taeja recalled Fallon calling him Strap before when they were at the restaurant. *The dude at the restaurant said his name was Cash... And I heard Damien call D 'Ghost' once before...*

"What else do you know?!" she demanded urgently. "Why do you think it was them?!"

"We saw them niggas leave with her. Put two and two together, ma."

"The police said nobody saw them leave with anyone," Taeja reasoned. "They couldn't even find any video surveillance."

Jimmy looked at her like it was common sense. "Cash owns that club. Slick ass motherfucker."

"I can't believe this," she muttered to herself. Taeja didn't want to jump to conclusions but how could she not? *That's definitely them, but... Is it really true?*

"Thank you for all the information, Jimmy. I really appreciate it."

"Ay, can a nigga get your number, at least?"

"Let me get yours," Taeja suggested. "I may need to call you and ask more questions later."

Jimmy looked at her seriously. "Leave that shit alone, ma. It happened months ago. The shit is dead." He started walking off. "I'm not getting involved. Matter fact, pretend we ain't even have this conversation."

Chapter 17

Cash sped down the highway with a million thoughts racing through his mind. He'd just left Kaleesha's house after she'd insisted she had something important to tell him. He hadn't understood why she couldn't tell him over the phone, but when he arrived it all made sense.

"Shan-Shan said Daddy was a bad man and bad things happen to bad people…" Monet's voice was shaking as she spoke. "S-sh-she pointed the gun at Daddy and-and it made a loud noise! Daddy couldn't get up! He needed help but Shan-shan said we can't call 911 cuz he's a bad man."

Cash was still tripping over that shit! *Kids Monet's age can't make shit like this up.*

He thought about the way his goddaughter had been shaking and crying hysterically. It had taken her several minutes just to form a coherent sentence. *She was so damn scared…* Cash hated to see kids like that. He'd done a lot of shit he wasn't proud of, but he'd never fucked with children.

I don't know if Monet was more fucked up over Outlaw dying or Shantreis threatening her... Cash doubted Shantreis would put her hands on the girl, but on second thought... *That bitch was bold as fuck. She was confident Monet wouldn't say shit.*

When Ghost first told him he'd figured it to be pure bullshit. He claimed to have seen Outlaw's body in the trunk but when Cash came over, it was inside the house. Shit wasn't completely adding up but before the end of the night, he was going to get all the answers he was looking for.

I dare Shantreis to lie about any of it. There were a few more things he'd looked into and it seemed like everything was coming back with Shantreis's name attached. *That bitch had really been plottin' on a nigga. I wonder if Fallon knew about it...*

Speaking of Fallon, he hadn't heard shit else from her since their confrontation. Although she'd promised to send over the information for her doctor's appointment, she'd yet to do so. *That shit looks real funny.* Fallon denied everything Remy said, but Cash had expected her to. As far as Remy went, she liked to start shit but she had never lied about it.

All this fucking bullshit in my life, Cash thought, reflecting on his conversation with Remy earlier.

"She ain't pregnant, Cash! That bitch bought that fuckin' test off Craig's List!" Remy had insisted. *"I overheard Fallon telling Shantreis when I was at the store! She just wants you back and she'll do anything to get you!"*

"Remy, that shit doesn't make sense," Cash reasoned. *"What the fuck she gonna do when there ain't no fuckin' baby?"*

"C'mon, Cash, I know you ain't that naïve! Fallon already said she would fake a miscarriage if she wasn't," Remy schooled him.

"Knowing that bitch, she probably wouldn't do it like that though. At the end of the day, Cash, I know you still love her. I can see it in your eyes... You've called me 'Fallon' before when we fuckin'. I never said shit before but I'm tired of it." Her admission was pitiful, but true.

"I know how bad you want a family, Cash. Don't forget how you was thinking about marrying me when I had Niyah," she reminded him. *"All it takes is for you to slip up, sleep with that bitch again, and nut in her!* Then *she'll have a baby and you wouldn't even know she got over on yo' ass!"*

Remy's eyes softened as she grasped his hand. *"I'm just tellin' you cuz you my nigga. I don't want you to get hurt again. Or get trapped by that bitch. I know she's been fuckin' with Strap, too."*

Cash was quiet. He'd never told her but he knew it didn't take long for gossip to spread in the streets. His workers knew not to say shit about it to his face but he couldn't stop them from talking behind his back. The humiliation hit so hard sometimes. It made him wish he had killed them off that morning, or at least forced them to move.

"She could get pregnant by him and say it's yours if she wants you bad enough." Remy sighed sadly, her mood mirroring his. *"Just be careful, bae. Find out for sure."*

If she's right about this shit I just might need to wife her ass, Cash thought snapping back to reality.

It was ironic how Remy was the only one that understood the meaning of loyalty. Apparently it was a word consisting of seven random letters that didn't mean shit to anyone else. *Shantreis murdered a nigga that always looked out for her hoe ass... Fallon slept with my blood and* still *with him... Strap and Ghost bit the muthafuckin' hand that fed them...*

If Fallon really did buy a test from somebody... I'll wanna strangle that bitch. I spared her last time but this time? Hell no! Cash shook his head. A part of him *knew* Fallon was probably lying. She'd looked too nervous when he asked and overall conflicted over what to say. Still, another part of him just *knew* she wouldn't lie about something serious like that. The old Fallon was still in there somewhere, right?

It's funny how you can be with somebody for three years and not really know them. I'm a' find out though, Cash thought. If Fallon was indeed lying to him then he was cutting her ass off for good—her and Strap. He'd agreed to tolerate Strap, but that condition existed only with a baby in the picture. Without one, there was no need to fuck with them anyway. They couldn't do shit for him and never had.

Cash turned off his lights as he prepared to pull into Shantreis's driveway. The ride over had taken him less than the usual thirty minutes. He attributed that to all the heavy shit on his mind as well as his lead foot.

"A'ight. Let's see what's really good," Cash said to himself as he removed his Smith & Wesson from his lap.

Shantreis glared at her cell phone as it went off for the tenth time. It was Blaze's usual routine as of late. He would keep calling her until she eventually cut her phone off.

She rolled her eyes before reluctantly answering the call. "Stop callin' me, muthafucka!" she demanded, preparing to hang up.

"Damn! Wait, Treis!" Blaze pleaded. "How long is you gonna ignore me? This shit is childish!"

Shantreis looked at the phone incredulously. "Nigga, are you seriously callin' me childish?! This from the bitch made nigga that wanted me so bad he had to trap my ass?"

"You can't abort our baby, Shantreis!"

"Nigga, I can do whatever the fuck I want. *You* did."

"You know that's not fair! I was just fuckin' with you! You know I wouldn't do no shit like that," he denied. "I just— Listen, *please* keep our baby!"

Shantreis could hear the desperation in his voice but she knew he wasn't sincere. *Lyin' ass!* She'd seen plenty niggas lie for the sake of saving their own asses when she was dealing with Outlaw. *He'd say whatever to get me to keep the baby.* "Bye, nigga! Don't call me no more!"

This time she didn't wait for his response before disconnecting the call. Finding Blaze's name in her contact list as 'Bitch Ass Blaze', she blocked his number. *I should've been did this.* Returning to the Home Screen of her phone, she gazed at her wallpaper. It was a picture of her last ultrasound.

Although Shantreis told Blaze she was aborting their child, she'd only said it because she was angry. After she'd had a moment to calm down and think about it, she couldn't bring herself to do it. Blaze would end up finding out one day that she actually had the baby but it wouldn't be any time soon.

Knock, Knock!

Shantreis looked up from her place on the bed. *Who the hell is it?* She sighed. *I swear to God that if Blaze brought his dumb ass over here...* She trudged down the stairs and to the front door. While walking, she made sure not to look over in the empty living room. Although there were no longer any traces of Outlaw's blood there, in her mind she would always have that visual image. It made her shudder.

I can't wait until this shit is sold and I can buy a new house. She'd thought to stay in a hotel but she hated to waste money. On top of that, Shantreis doubted a hotel would have enough space for all of her things. Staying here was more convenient.

"Hey, Cash," she said uneasily as she opened the door, surprised to see him there. It was nearing five thirty and the sun was starting to set. "What's up?"

"Mind if I come inside?" he asked politely.

"I don't really have any furniture for us to sit on... I only have my bed upstairs. It might be better if we sat out on the porch swing," Shantreis suggested, trying to read him.

His eyes scanned past her, noticing that the house was empty. In his haste, Cash hadn't even noticed the 'Sale Pending' sign in the yard. "It'll be quick," he assured her, pushing past her into the house.

Shantreis stood there nervously, debating her next move. *This shit don't seem right. Is he up to something or am I just paranoid?* She looked back at him. *Should I make a run for it?* Her keys were upstairs in her purse and her car was parked in the garage. *Cash crazy, but he ain't like Ghost. He won't assault my ass in public. It's a few neighbors outside watering their lawn so—*

"*Close* the door," he demanded, interrupting her thoughts. *"Now!* If you thinkin' about runnin', *don't*. I'll grab yo' ass before you make it out."

Cash stood directly behind her, less than a foot away. Although he could easily shut it himself, he wanted *Shantreis* to do it. It was the simple matter of exerting his power over her at the moment.

Shantreis obeyed him, closing the door lightly. Turning around and noticing the gun pointed at her, she tried to hide the fear coursing through her veins. She observed the silencer attached to the end. *What the hell has he heard?* Her eyes raced back and forth from his gun to his face.

"Sit down on the floor and talk to me," Cash ordered calmly, nodding his head in the direction he wanted her. "Put yo' fuckin' hands behind ya head."

She nodded slowly, doing as she was told. "Cash, I don't know what you heard but—"

"Shut the fuck up!" For several minutes he just stared at her viciously, shaking his head. The pitiful look on her face pissed him off. He walked closer, his eyes and gun remained locked on her.

Shantreis shivered slightly, unnerved by his silence. She would feel a little better if he said something… anything! *What the fuck is he gonna do? He shouldn't know shit! But he's got to if he doin' all this…*

"How the fuck could you kill the nigga that did everything for yo' scandalous ass?!" Cash boomed. "You thought I wouldn't find out, bitch?! You threatenin' lil' kids and shit?!"

Fuck. She felt her blood run cold. *That's how he found out. Monet must've told him everything…* She didn't answer, instead keeping her eyes on the gun.

"Worthless ass bitch!" Cash grabbed her hair forcefully, almost ripping it from the roots then knocked her face down to the floor like she was a rag doll. Shantreis cried out in pain, massaging her head as she noticed some strands break off and fall to the floor.

"Cash, please!" she begged. Tears flowed freely down her face as she started to shake. "Hear me out!!!"

"What?!" Cash barked. He lifted his hand, backhanding her with the butt of his gun. Shantreis's neck twisted violently from the force. The sound that came from her wasn't human as blood poured from her mouth.

Hovering over her, he placed the tip of the gun to her temple. "What the fuck you got to say? Ain't shit you can say to save ya life but go ahead!"

Fuck it, Shantreis thought, sucking up her tears. She knew Cash meant business. Mercy was a word that wasn't associated with how he handled things. *If I'm just gon die anyway… It won't be like a punk.* She was still trembling but she'd managed to compose herself slightly. Regaining her pride, she started, "Yeah I did it. If I had to do it over again, I would!"

His finger wrapped around the trigger.

She glared at him unflinchingly. "I did the same shit you or Outlaw would've done if some muthafucka tried to *kill* you or your *baby*! If you can't understand that, nigga, fuck you!"

Shantreis took a deep breath and closed her eyes, apologizing silently to her unborn child. *I'm sorry you won't get a chance to see this world, but we'll go somewhere better. I promise.* She embraced her stomach tightly as she waited for the inevitable.

In that moment, everything went black.

Chapter 18

I don't know why I can't leave this girl alone. Strap swore to himself that he wouldn't continue fucking with Taeja after knowing she was Vanessa's sister, but yet here he was. He'd just pulled up to her apartment, preparing to take her out to Regal Cinemas to see a movie.

Strap rapped on her front door before placing his hands inside his Rag & Bone leather jacket. While he sincerely liked Taeja, he also felt slightly indebted to her. *Whatever I can do for her, I will.* He felt he owed her that much, even if they didn't end up working out in the long run. Maybe his logic was fucked up, but he couldn't leave her alone if he wanted to. She was the only female since Fallon that he'd actually connected with. He would be a fool to let her go. Strap thought so, anyway.

Taeja opened the door slightly. Strap could see she had the security chain on.

"What's wrong? You ain't dressed yet?" Strap asked.

"No," she answered curtly.

"Malaysia can't watch Kai? I can pick up a Redbox then—"

"I just want you to answer a question... honestly," Taeja said. Her voice was shaky as she continued to peer through the small gap.

"What's up?"

"Did you have something to do with my sister being killed?"

"What the fuck?" The surprise was apparent on Strap's face. "Where that shit come from?"

"Answer the question, *Strap.*" She used his street name for emphasis. It was her subtle way of making him aware she knew more than he thought.

The fuck has she heard? Strap wondered. "Can I come in and talk to you?"

"Why?! So you can kill me too?!" Taeja practically screamed.

"Taeja, are you fuckin' kiddin' me?! I wouldn't kill *anybody,* least of all, *you!* Where the fuck is you gettin' this shit from?!" He blew his breath exasperatedly. "You don't know what the fuck you're talkin' about! You're just causin' a fuckin' scene!" He looked over at her neighbor who had just come outside to take out the trash. "Damn!"

"Tell me, Damien! The truth! Because I *will* find out!"

Strap sighed and leaned against the side of the door. "Come out to the car if you wanna talk... Or call my phone or some shit cuz I ain't havin' this conversation with you outside. It's cold as fuck too."

Placing his hands back inside his jacket, he made his way back to his car. He didn't know if Taeja would take him up on his offer, but he wanted a chance to explain himself.

Even though I'm just gonna lie to her anyway, he thought shamefully.

No sooner than he'd gotten inside his car did he see Taeja descending the stairs.

Are you kiddin' me? he thought with disbelief. *A butcher's knife?*

Taeja opened the passenger door and sat down with an attitude. A million thoughts were racing through her mind. Although she'd told herself to *ask* him instead of accusing him, she forgot the moment he showed up.

"Taeja, put the knife away," he tried to reason with her. "Ain't no need for all that shit."

"Don't tell me what to do!" she screeched hysterically. "What happened, Damien? I know you left with my sister."

Strap nodded slowly. "You're right. I did."

Oh God, Taeja thought. She couldn't suppress the squeal that left her lips. "How could you?!" Impulsively she went to hit him, oblivious of the knife still in her right hand.

Quickly Strap grabbed both of her wrists tightly before she could make contact with his skin. "Put it down, Taeja, and hear me out cuz it ain't shit like you think!" He forced the knife out of her hands until it dropped at his feet. Still he refused to release his hold on her.

"I hate you! Stop it!" she screamed, moving wildly. She couldn't hear a word over her own cries. To Taeja, there was nothing else to explain. He had basically admitted his guilt to her. Everything added up. "You bastard! Let go!"

"Taeja, I *didn't* kill your sister!" Strap stared her directly in the eyes, silently begging for her to believe him.

"I *said* let go! You're hurting me!"

"Nah! Not until you listen to me and calm the fuck down!" He loosened his grip slightly. "It's true I left with her but that's it! We got a hotel room but I ain't fuck. Her nigga kept calling her and she left! That's it!"

"No! Jimmy said—" she started, forgetting the man's plea to leave him out of it. "They were supposed to rob someone that night but—"

"That ain't got shit to do with me, Tae. I ain't sayin' that nigga lyin' to you but he don't know what the hell he talkin' about either."

"Why didn't you tell me you knew her then?!"

"What difference would it have made? I didn't know she was your sister until I saw the picture of y'all! I knew Vanessa for all of what—an hour or some shit?"

Taeja searched his eyes, looking for the truth. Was it really as he claimed or was he lying? "Damien, I really need to know," she begged through red-rimmed eyes. "Is there something else you're not telling me? If you didn't do it, do you know who did?"

Strap sighed before giving her the best response he could. "That's all I know, Tae. You gotta believe me. But if you don't or you still have doubts, then maybe we need to go our separate ways. She was your *sister*. Why would I try to be in yo' life if I did some foul shit like that?"

"Swear to God?"

"Taeja…"

"Just swear, Damien!"

"I swear," he replied.

Taeja studied him for a few more moments before releasing a shaky sigh of relief. Wiping the tears from her eyes, she sank back into the soft leather of his seats.

"Okay… I'm gonna believe you then." *Please, Lord,* she prayed desperately. *Let it be the truth.* She really liked Strap, but if he had anything to do with her sister… *Help me, God, but I would kill him with my bare hands.* Taeja and Vanessa hadn't been the closest of sisters, but they were blood nonetheless, and loved each other.

I'm going to Hell, Strap thought. *But what the fuck was I supposed to say? 'Taeja, my brother killed your sister but only because she was grimy as hell and it was kill or be killed?' Yeah fuckin' right... I did the right thing.*

"Can we reschedule though?" Taeja asked with a half-smile, knocking him from his thoughts. "I look a mess and..."

"Yeah." Strap nodded. "That's cool."

Taeja started out the car but stopped to look back at Strap. "I'm uh... Sorry for the way I acted earlier. I just thought—"

"Don't be, Taeja." He shook his head. "Don't be..."

C ash stared at Shantreis's limp body thinking about what she'd told him. *Damn. Outlaw tried to kill her? Over what?*

Outlaw hadn't breathed so much of a word of it to him, but if Cash had to guess it was probably dealing with Blaze. He'd warned her to leave that nigga alone but it was obvious she hadn't heeded his advice.

Is it that nigga's baby then? Looking at Shantreis now, he could see how much rounder her face was and the unmistakable spread of her nose. *Damn...*

Monet had mentioned Outlaw giving Shantreis a 'whupping' but he hadn't thought about it until after Shantreis made her confession.

"Ay!" Cash yelled, smacking her face lightly. "Get up!"

Her words had really connected with him. She was right. He would've killed any nigga or bitch that would've tried to take his life. Still, there was something about killing a pregnant woman that he just couldn't do.

Ghost would probably call me soft, Cash thought with a slight chuckle but just as soon as the thought came, it disappeared. Ghost had been distant in his thoughts recently, but deep down inside, he missed his brazen little brother.

"Shantreis!" he tried again. Instead of shooting her as he'd originally intended, he just knocked her out while he sorted his thoughts.

"Whaa?" she cried out, disoriented.

"I'm a' let you keep your life, a'ight?"

Shantreis nodded her head unsteadily. She was still in a daze and didn't fully understand what was going on.

"But stay the fuck away from Monet, got it? And if you *ever* think about comin' after me on some revenge shit, I will torture yo' ass to the point that you'll *beg* for me to kill you!" Cash snarled.

"Yes…"

"I'm glad we came to an understanding." He stood up slowly and left just as quietly as he'd come. *Now I gotta finish this shit with Fallon.*

Chapter 19

"When it's for real, it's forever. So don't forget about us," Fallon sung along brightly with the Mariah Carey song playing in her head. She'd just stepped out of the bathtub in an uncharacteristically good mood. Only one man was responsible for that.

Cash.

Fallon rubbed lotion onto her legs with a smile. He'd called her only a few minutes ago asking if he could come "chill". She agreed with no questions asked although she'd found his request strange.

It was nearing eight o' clock at night. *We haven't spoken since that day at the restaurant when he told me about that bullshit Remy said,* she thought bitterly. *I guess she was lying about the recording since he didn't say anything about that.* She sighed in relief.

Fallon still hadn't gotten back with Cash about her doctor's appointment. She would avoid it as long as possible until she could think of a feasible excuse. The light bleeding that she'd experienced had stopped, but she didn't know what to make of it.

Oh well. I'm sure he's not coming all the way over here to talk about that. But I wonder why he wanted to come over anyway. Does he know that me and Strap are done? She shook her head. *How would he know that? I'm sure he hasn't spoken to Strap and I haven't told him...*

Fallon quickly spritzed on some perfume and hurriedly tried to apply her makeup. It was laughable the lengths she was going to just to see Cash, but she wanted to look her best. *I have to be prepared for anything.* Giving herself an onceover in the mirror, Fallon smiled, satisfied with her reflection.

Knock knock!

"Damn it," she cursed, not having a chance to pick out anything to wear. She looked down at the silk robe she was wearing. It was turquoise blue with kimono sleeves and stopped at her thigh. *Oh well.*

Fallon took a deep breath before making her way to the door. "Hey, Cash," she greeted nervously. "Come in." She was barely able to make eye contact with him after inhaling the strong scent of his Versace cologne. He smelled so good that it made her knees weak.

Even though it hadn't been long since she'd last seen him, having Cash standing in her doorway seemed unreal. He still towered over her by a full foot, making her feel tiny in comparison, but it was a turn on. She wanted him to demonstrate his physical advantage over her. She bit her lip as her mind took her back to how it felt to be pressed underneath his body... with a few stray strands of his dreads dangling in her face as he pushed in and out of her...

Why did I fuck that up? Fallon wondered to herself, still admiring him. His attire was simple, as it usually was. A black v-neck, Fendi belt, and Balmain jeans. Everything hung off his body perfectly.

"You heard me?" Cash asked, snapping her from her thoughts. He looked at her strangely, taking in her full face of makeup and short, kimono robe. "You was goin' out somewhere? Got a date?"

"No!" She blushed, feeling slightly silly. "I just…"

"You did that shit for me?"

"I… uh…" Fallon stammered embarrassedly.

"Here." Cash handed her the small plastic bag he'd been holding. She hadn't even noticed it until that moment.

"What is…?" Her voice trailed off as she peered at the contents of the bag. *Clearblue Advanced Pregnancy Test With Weeks Estimator?! And it's two of them in here? What the hell?* "Cash, are you kiddin' me?"

"Nah." He took her by the hand, leading her to the bathroom. "Go ahead."

"In front of you?!" she asked incredulously.

"Leave the door open," Cash instructed, noting the tense expression on her face. His conversation with Remy really made him think. The fact that Fallon had been less than forthcoming with the details of her upcoming doctor's appointment put the nail in the coffin. Cash was 99% certain Fallon wasn't pregnant, but he had to see it with his own eyes.

The shit obvious enough. She a lyin' ass bitch, he thought hatefully. Cash was ready to call her out on her shit. *Why do you keep doin' this kinda shit, shawty?* He gazed at her pensively. He had to admit seeing Fallon dressed so seductively made his dick jump slightly but he'd never been the type to think with his little head. *Beautiful and scandalous...*

"What do you think I'm gonna do in there?!" Fallon stalled. *How the hell am I gonna get myself out of this one?* She was going to go with the excuse that her pregnancy test had made a mistake, but the look on Cash's face told her that he wasn't going to go for that. *I'd rather die than tell him where that test came from!* "You're treating me like I'm getting tested for drugs or something!"

"Fallon," he said impatiently. "Go 'head on, now!"

"What is this supposed to prove? I already showed you a test!"

"Remy said the shit was fake!"

"You trust everything she tells you?!" Fallon spat back, hurt that he had so much faith in another woman.

"I don't trust *no* bitch!" Cash clarified. "But I know what I heard."

"W-wh-what you heard? What do you mean?" Her voice faltered with panic. *He already knows... Remy* did *send him the recording. God no! Then why are we doing this?* she wondered. *Is he really that cruel that he has to see it too?*

"You got some shit to confess or you still gon' say Remy lyin' on you?"

"Fuck her!" Fallon screamed. "I'll take your stupid ass test but if—and that's *if*—it's negative, that doesn't mean a thing! Pregnancy tests give wrong results all the time. I didn't lie!"

He sighed angrily. "So what you gonna say if this one comes up negative? You just gon' keep lyin' about it?"

"Fuck you, Cash! I hope I'm not pregnant cuz I wouldn't wanna be stuck with your ass for eighteen years any damn way!"

"Yeah. Okay," he said unconvinced. "That's why you bought a test from a bitch off Craig's List." He nodded. "That's why you let me come over to your house and answered the door half-naked even though you got a nigga."

"I don't have a nigga! I'm not dealing with Strap anymore but it's not like that's any of your business!" Fallon was close to tears but she wouldn't give him the satisfaction. She'd forgotten how cold he could be, mainly because he rarely showed that side of himself to her. At least, not until late.

"Fallon, I ain't 'bout to sit here and argue with yo' ass. Take the test or just admit you a fuckin' liar!"

Fallon narrowed her eyes before going into the bathroom, slamming the door behind her.

Cash sighed. It hadn't been his intention to come over yelling and cursing at her, but he couldn't help it. The only thing she seemed to do consistency was piss him off. *I don't know what the hell I'm gonna do when I see that negative ass test... I probably just need to be thankful I ain't gotta deal with her ass no more.*

Still, he couldn't help but feel a tinge of sadness. Although the timing wasn't the best, Cash had been excited about the prospect of having a child. Fallon was a lot of things, but he was sure she would be a fantastic mother. She was the only female he'd ever envisioned as the mother of his child. *It wasn't supposed to be like this though...*

Hearing the toilet flush, he looked up as Fallon exited the bathroom.

"Happy now?" She threw the test at him carelessly but Cash still managed to catch it. "It'll show the results in three minutes. Now get the hell out of my house, Cash, before I call the police!"

"The police? You jokin'?" he sneered as he stared at the hourglass forming on the test. "You think I'm a' hurt you or some shit after I find out you lied?"

She shrugged. "This is the only reason you came over, right? So you got what you wanted and you can go."

Cash nodded dismissively before standing up to leave. "You got it, shawty."

Cash sat in his Bentley with the test sitting on his lap. He was still sitting in the parking lot of Fallon's apartment complex. There was one minute left before the results would show up. He stared at the display intently, urging it to hurry.

Came up, that's all me… Stay true, that's all me…

Cash glanced at his ringing cell phone. Remy's name was on the caller ID. "Whassup?"

"You still coming over?" Remy asked Cash eagerly.

"Shit… I don't know. I'm dealin' with this shit with Fallon right now."

"Did she deny what I told you? That bitch ain't pregnant is she?! I knew it though! I know the recording I sent ain't come out good, but I'm tryna tell you she admitted it!"

Cash was silent.

"Cash? Hello? You still there?" Remy called out.

"Ay, I'm a' call you back," he told her, not waiting for a response before disconnecting the call. The results were there… clear as day.

Cash exited his car, making his way back to her apartment. He didn't give a damn what Fallon said, they were gonna talk about this.

Knock, knock!

"Cash, if that's you—" he could hear her voice from inside.

"Just open the damn door, Fallon! We need to talk about this shit."

"I don't want to!" Fallon insisted childishly. "What else is there to say?!"

"I ain't goin' nowhere until you open the door! Now either you can or I *will*."

"What are you gonna do—kick my door in?!"

Cash sighed, fed up with Fallon talking to him like he was some sort of crazy ass nigga. *Is this what she thinks of me? Or does she just know that she did some trifling ass shit so that's why she scared?* "That's not what I meant and you know it."

"Whatever you have to say, you can say it outside," she asserted.

"Fine," he started. "Look, I just wanted to apologize for the way I came at you. I meant what I told you before, I'm gonna be there for you and my seed—"

"What?" Fallon questioned. Her heart felt like it was about to burst out of her chest. Was he playing a joke on her? All of a sudden she opened the door and snatched the test from his hand.

Pregnant. 3+ weeks, she read silently. Tears of joy sprang to her eyes. Just that quickly all the anger she'd felt towards him earlier dissipated. *I can't believe it.*

"You look surprised," Cash joked.

"No." She straightened herself up and wiped at her eyes. Inwardly she thanked God for working a miracle. "I'm happy you know the truth now… I hated that you doubted me." She couldn't help herself when she reflexively hugged him.

Cash stood frozen for a moment. The sweet scent of her Flowerbomb perfume wafted up his nostrils. The feel of her soft, small body pressed against his caused him to momentarily forget their past relationship issues. All bullshit aside, he knew he still loved her. The fact that she was having his child only cultivated his love for her.

Be that as it may, the weight of Fallon's betrayal was still heavy even though some had been lifted with time. To take his mind off her, Cash spent some of his free time with Remy, but their time together only served as a reminder of why he'd never settled down and wifed her... She just wasn't Fallon. Fallon was like a damn magnet, she kept pulling him back to her. He didn't even completely understand that shit.

This love shit is complicated as fuck, Cash thought. *Can I really forgive her for* fucking *my brother?* His resolve weakened unconsciously as his arms went to wrap around her, but Fallon jerked back before he could.

"Sorry. I just got a little..." she apologized.

"You good," Cash assured her, fighting the urge to embrace her tightly. "Let me know when your doctor's appointment is... I'll take you, a'ight?"

Fallon nodded. "Okay."

Chapter 20

5 *Months Later*

"I can't believe it!" Fallon gushed. "These are *our* babies!" She stared down at the 4-D Ultrasound in her hand. "Wow. I still can't believe we're having twins!"

When Fallon first heard the news, she had been in denial. It was a possibility she hadn't completely ruled out, but she'd still thought the likelihood of having twins was slim. All that changed when the doctor heard two heartbeats.

Two boys, she thought happily. Initially she had been slightly disappointed that she wasn't having a girl, but seeing their little faces on the ultrasound quickly erased those sentiments. Fallon would love them regardless.

Fallon was reaching the six month mark, but pregnancy definitely suited her. She had the unmistakable glow. Her hair now swept halfway down her back in stylish layers. Despite carrying an extra thirty pounds on her frame, Fallon still kept her appearance up. She was honestly enjoying her pregnancy.

Cash grinned proudly, glancing over slightly as he pulled his car out of the doctor's office parking lot. He'd been accompanying Fallon to her appointments from day one, as promised. With each passing day, a lot of his anger towards her subsided. They were getting along, but their relationship was strictly platonic despite the growing sexual tension between them. Getting back together made sense, but neither had made a step in that direction... yet.

"Damon and Montrez Hardy," Fallon beamed, staring at the ultrasound again. They'd decided to name the boys after Cash.

"You hungry?" Cash asked.

"Not really. I had a—" Fallon's eyes widened in alarm. "Oh my God, Cash!"

"What?!" He looked at her worriedly. "What's wrong?"

She reached for his right hand and brought it to her stomach. "They moved! They're kicking me!" she exclaimed excitedly. "Do you feel it?"

Cash smiled. "Yeah I feel it." Fallon was still chattering on excitedly about it but he was no longer listening. Feeling the twins' move made him think about the future.

I know I'm always gonna be a part of their life, but I'm probably gonna miss a lot of shit, he thought unhappily. Fallon had her own place, as did he. Without a question of a doubt, the twins' would spend most of their time at Fallon's house. *I might miss their first steps or first word...*

Shit. We was supposed to be married by now. We doin' shit backwards as hell... He gazed at her bare ring finger. *I wonder where she put the ring.*

"Cash, did you hear me?"

"Nah." He snapped out his daze. "What'd you say?"

"I got a text from Shantreis! She's having the baby!!!"

"**A**rrrgghhh!!!" Shantreis screamed as she pushed with everything in her.

"Breathe," the nurse instructed. "Now push again."

"Oh God!" Shantreis closed her eyes and pushed, trying desperately to remember the breathing exercises she'd been taught during Lamaze class.

Blaze, where the fuck are you?! she wondered, imagining him standing next to her, holding her hand and soothing her with comforting words.

Although Shantreis put on an icy façade in front of Blaze, she still appreciated his presence. No matter how much she tried to push him away, he stayed persistently by her side. He believed her hormones were the cause of her less than pleasant behavior and he was right. After much persuading and apologizing, he convinced her to move back in—at least until she had the baby. Shantreis agreed, but Blaze hoped she would stay on a more permanent basis.

Nigga, you were supposed to be here! I bet them muthafuckas wouldn't let him off work early.

Blaze had recently gotten promoted to Operations Supervisor so it was harder for him to take off, especially now that he was working the day shift. Still, she'd hoped he could be there.

"You doin' real good, baby," Shantreis could hear Blaze say, but she wasn't sure if it was her imagination or not.

Opening her eyes, she saw he was real. A slight smile formed on her face.

"We can see the head," the doctor announced. "One more big push and that's it."

Shantreis took a deep breath before pushing again, gritting her teeth.

"You did it!" they announced in unison.

"Thank God," she moaned, throwing her head back in exhaustion.

Blaze kissed the top of her sweaty forehead. "Good job, baby."

"Here's your daughter," the doctor said, handing over a tiny, light brown baby swaddled in a hospital provided blanket. "Seven pounds even."

A few weeks ago they'd learned their son was actually a daughter. Despite Blaze's initial desire for a son, he was still happy.

Ashanti Jacolyn Teasley, Shantreis thought. Blaze wanted the baby to have his last name, but she wasn't going for that. At the end of the day, they weren't married and bigger than that, who knew if Ashanti was even Blaze's daughter?

"It don't matter cuz no matter what, she's mine," Blaze had told her when she'd voiced her concerns. "I'm gonna sign the certificate. That nigga dead anyway. You don't gotta go through this shit alone."

His words made her smile. *It's still some good niggas in this world,* she thought. Not too many would be willing to take care of a child that might not be theirs. Blaze was different. *He's what a real nigga supposed to be like.* Shantreis would probably never tell him but she was grateful for him staying by her side.

"She looks just like you," Blaze commented with a smile. "Beautiful."

Shantreis beamed. "I think you're right." Ashanti had a head full of black hair with chubby cheeks and small lips that were already scowling.

"She gonna have an attitude like yours, too."

"Shut up, boy."

"Oh my God, Shantreis!" Fallon squealed excitedly as she entered the room. "Is that her? Is that Baby Shan?"

Shantreis rolled her eyes. "There you go with that 'baby' shit," she joked, remembering how Fallon referred to her own unborn children as 'Baby Damon' and 'Baby Montrez'. "Just call her Ashanti."

"Lemme hold her," Fallon cooed, ignoring her best friend. Gently she took the baby into her arms, rocking her back and forth. "She's so cute! Y'all did good."

"Thanks."

"Oh! Let me show you my boys." Handing the baby to Blaze, she reached into her purse for the ultrasound images. "Look! They look just like Cash."

Shantreis nodded her head with a smile. Cash wasn't her favorite person since their run in five months ago, but she understood his position. It was the way of the streets. She was just grateful she'd gotten yet another chance to be there for her daughter.

"I can't believe you still fuckin' wit' Taeja!" Ghost shook his head with a smile.

Strap grinned. He wouldn't admit it aloud, but so was he… not that he was complaining. "Shit, nigga. That's how it's supposed to be when you got a good one. You keep her."

Ghost nodded. "She must got some good pussy. Got a nigga buyin' hundred dollar cakes and shit." He referred to the huge, pink princess cake they'd just picked up from Edible Art Bakery.

It was Kairi's first birthday. Strap wanted to make sure it was special. Taeja had already warned him not to go overboard but he didn't pay her any mind. He loved the little girl like his own and spoiled her rotten. Likewise, Kairi was crazy about her 'Sap'. She couldn't properly say his name yet, and that was as close as she could get.

It was funny how so much could change in five, short months. Strap's life was going well—much better than he could've ever expected. After he and Taeja had almost fallen out over Vanessa's death, Strap kept his distance from her. His conscience had worn him down, but Taeja was persistent. She was an infectious person to be around. Shaking her wasn't as easy as he'd thought it would be.

Strap spent most of his life as a loner, at least when it came to females. It was only after dealing with Fallon and Taeja that he found himself changing. Maybe Ghost was right when he'd taunt him about being a 'sucka for love'. In the end, he decided to push his guilt to the back of his mind and continued to see Taeja. He couldn't have been happier with his decision.

Everything happens for a reason, Strap thought. He wished the circumstances could've been different but it was what it was. He could honestly say Taeja made him a better person. He'd already started attending Shaw University and had a 3.2 GPA with her help. She encouraged him whenever he felt like quitting, acting as his own personal cheerleader.

Thanks to all the love she'd shown him, Strap took the money he'd saved and invested over the years to purchase a new Craftsman style home in Parker Falls. Taeja hadn't officially moved in with him, but she was over so much that he considered it her home, too. Besides, with four bedrooms and five bathrooms, the house was much too big for him alone. Sometimes Ghost would crash at his place when Malaysia kicked him out, but lately those incidents were few and far in-between.

"You can have that family man shit," Ghost said, knocking his twin from his thoughts.

"I heard Malaysia want a baby," Strap mentioned, knowing his comment would get under his brother's skin.

"I don't give a fuuuckkk," he drawled, his Southern accent on full display. "I don't want no fuckin' kids. Ain't 'bout to make me soft like you. Got us in this damn Party City and shit."

They were waiting on the balloons Strap had ordered before they headed back to Kairi's party. Taeja was running late from her new job at Allscripts so Strap offered to take care of the cake while she tended to things at home. Instead of having a celebration at Chuck E. Cheese or any other typical place, they were having it at their house. Strap rented Inflatables, pony rides, and more shit that Kairi was unlikely to remember as she grew up.

"Here you go, sir," the cashier said, handing over fifteen helium-filled balloons. "Sorry about the wait."

"No problem," Strap told her coolly. They made their way out the door, heading back to the car when he spotted a familiar face walking in their direction.

Cash? Strap hadn't spoken to his older brother since the restaurant incident. *Come to think of it, I ain't even address him then...* He'd wanted to get up with Cash and talk about everything, but he didn't know how. He didn't know how the conversation would be received either. At the end of the day, Strap decided to leave it alone. He missed his brother—after all, Cash practically raised them. He was the only male role model they'd had growing up. Not talking to him felt strange, but Strap had grown accustomed to it.

I ain't got no beef with that nigga, but who knows how the fuck he feels. Should I just act like I don't see him? He glanced over at Ghost, but his face was unreadable. Strap knew the bounty had been called off months ago, but when it came to the Hardy brothers, shit was unpredictable.

"What's up?" Cash greeted, breaking the ice as the distance between them shortened.

"What's up, man?" Strap said, half surprised but accepting his brother's outstretched hand.

Ghost nodded his head in acknowledgement. "Wassup, Cash?"

Damn, Strap thought. He hadn't expected Ghost to speak. *Almost feels like old times.* "Congratulations," Strap added, realizing it was something he'd never told his brother.

Cash smiled proudly. "'Preciate it, man. But ay, I'm a' holla at y'all later."

Strap nodded. *Guess that beefin' shit is done.* He gazed back at his brother's retreating figure with a smile. He doubted things would go back exactly as they were before, but it was a start in the right direction.

Chapter 21

"She is just *soooo* cute," Fallon continued. She'd been telling Cash about Shantreis's daughter since he'd picked her up from WakeMed. "I wish you could've seen her."

"She look like Outlaw?" Cash asked somberly.

"She looks like Shantreis," she admitted softly, feeling insensitive for having brought it up. "I don't know if she's Outlaw's daughter or not. Blaze is claiming her as his child. I don't even think they're going to do a paternity test. He signed the birth certificate earlier, too."

Cash grunted in response. He didn't regret sparing Shantreis's life after knowing her circumstances, but he wished his nigga could've been around. *All the bullshit aside, he would a' still loved that little girl regardless of how scandalous her damn momma was.*

"But where are we going?" Fallon asked, finally noticing they weren't heading in the direction of her apartment. Instead they were going towards Wakefield, where Cash lived.

"I got a surprise I wanna show you," he answered casually.

Fifteen minutes later they pulled up in front of his house.

It's been so long since I've been here, Fallon thought. *We really had some good times when I lived here…*

Cash walked around to open Fallon's car door and helped her out. "Close your eyes," he requested, placing his hands over her eyes to ensure she didn't peek.

"Okay," she said shakily, nervous about following his lead in her three-inch heels.

Effortlessly Cash guided her inside the house and down the hallway. When they reached a door at the end of the hall, he asked her to open her eyes.

"Oh my God, Cash!" Fallon cupped her hands over her mouth in disbelief. "This is beautiful."

Seeing the lavish baby room prepared for the twins brought tears to her eyes. The high ceilings had been painted to resemble the sky, complete with stars, clouds, and the moon, giving the room a serene feeling. The walls were a calming blue color with their sons' names printed tastefully along the side. Two circular cribs were spaced a couple of feet apart with plush, gold-tinged bedding. A glider chair sat in the corner with a changing table alongside the opposite wall.

"When did you…?" Fallon couldn't get the question out before she started sobbing uncontrollably.

Cash looked at her in confusion. He could tell these were no longer tears of joy, but of genuine sorrow. "What's wrong?"

"Cash, I'm so sorry I messed everything up… between us…" she bawled. "W-we were…" Once again she erupted into tears, unable to complete her sentence.

"Baby, stop cryin'." He wiped her tears away. "Listen, I did this because I want us to be a family… like we were supposed to be. I don't wanna be away from my sons. I want all *three* of y'all in my life."

Fallon sniffled, trying hard to compose herself. "It's only because of the twins though, right? You said you moved Remy in because of the baby… Is it really *me* you want to be with or would any girl pregnant with your child have gotten this privilege?"

"Listen, Fallon," Cash said, lifting her chin to look at him directly. "Don't compare that shit cuz it ain't the same. You know I love you… I just hated what you did. That shit…" His voice trailed off. "It really fucked with a nigga. I'm a' keep it real wit' you though. I wouldn't have fucked with you again if you wasn't pregnant with my seed but I think shit happens for a reason.

"I want things to go back to the way they were before." Cash kissed her forehead tenderly. "I thought about the shit for a long time. What you said before was right. You fucked up before and so have I. Life's too short for the bullshit. Move back in." He kissed her lips softly, passionately, trying to ease any doubt she may have had. "Okay?"

"Okay," Fallon replied breathlessly, completely weak after the way he'd kissed her. It had been so long since she'd been kissed… since she'd been touched… She was extra sensitive to his every action.

Fallon pulled his body closer to hers, devouring his kisses greedily. "Oooh, Cash," she moaned against his lips in anticipation of what was to come.

"Damn, girl." Cash lifted her and carried her to his bedroom, laying her on the bed. Gently he removed her clothes, teasing her each time his fingers brushed across her skin.

"Please, baby…" Fallon begged, clad only in her bra and panties. "Put it in." She grinded against Cash, feeling her panties soak even more when he cupped her butt cheeks and massaged them gently.

Cash obliged her, savoring the way her tightness invited him in. As he moved in and out of her, he gazed into her ecstasy-filled eyes with pride. She was finally back in his arms again. "Is it mine?"

"Yes, Damontrez," she cried. "It's all yours."

A smile of satisfaction tugged at his lips from her confession. "Don't give my shit away again, got it?" Cash asked gruffly, pushing into her deeper to hit a new pleasure inducing spot.

"Yes… I swear I won't," Fallon shrieked with passion. "Never ever." She had gotten a second chance at true love and she wasn't going to lose it again. She couldn't wait to start a new life with her twin boys and her first love.

"I love you, Cash."

"I love you, too, Fallon."

THE END… or is it? Should I make a part 3? Let me know what you think:

You can reach me at:

Twitter: @Author_LoveNLee

Email: author_loven.lee@hotmail.com

Facebook: www.facebook.com/author.lovenlee

ALSO AVAILABLE FROM JME PUBLICATIONS

Already Taken by Love N. Lee

Beauty and the Thug by Love N. Lee

Cherish by Tihanna Peach

Love and the Streets by Love N. Lee

Love Hate Thing by Love N. Lee

Mine Games by Love N. Lee

Rap Star Wifeys: Miami Season 1 by Love N. Lee

Rap Star Wifeys: Miami Season 2 by Love N. Lee

She Can't Love You by Nicole Red

Street Love by Love N. Lee

Street Love 2 by Love N. Lee

Go to eepurl.com/ryocn to be added to JME Publications mailing list for exclusive sneak peeks, contests, and more!